In The End

By
J. Ann Royal

Disclaimer

This novel is a work of fiction

Dedication

For T,

who will look down from
the skies above - and laugh
once more. You are greatly
missed my friend.

jar

About the Author

After winning her first essay contest, Ann knew what she wanted to be as an adult. Since then, a list of accomplishments for writing and photography is included in her repertoire.

A Mississippi native who has had an active lifestyle of hiking, rock climbing, exploring unknown territories, and also becoming a crew chief for a hot air balloon company.

Look for announcements of future J. Ann Royal novels on www.tiktok.com/ @wanderingjournalist

TABLE OF CONTENTS

Chapter 1

Older, unkept homes on the left and mobile homes to my right, and I can visibly see my friend waving now. She motions to me with an all-too-common phrase, "Get out and stay awhile." Her hair is in disarray, and although it's midafternoon, Virginia is still in her nightgown. It's always nice to see that sweet smile, even when I know she has not been well lately. Declining health is taking a noticeable toll, as she no longer rises to greet me. This beautiful, full-of-life person can still out-talk and stand her ground against the toughest souls. I admired "Ginny" from the start of our friendship, but would readily admit that there were times I didn't understand her motives.

An emotional roller coaster most days, and picking unwarranted arguments with her husband were all too common. Had she always been unpredictable, or was it just in her to fight battles only to give them up at bedtime? Ginny could be the wench in this neighborhood, but also the culprit of misadventures to get her way about things. Intelligent, shrewd, and definitely knowledgeable about life is the best description for Ginny.

A local attorney had been her first beau, although no marriage came about before his death. Acquaintances described them as the attorney and his overruling legal secretary. I never met him, but I have imagined the love he must have had for her. Besides, not many Southern gentlemen would want a powerful woman in their lives, and certainly not one working for their law practice. Seeing photos of them together makes me smile, and I've teased her about her boots being bigger than his. And then her laughter comes with tears thrown in, and she shakes her fist toward the heavens in protest to him because he left her.

And then there was another gentleman who had caught her fancy. He had owned a "honky-tonk" type bar. Somewhere along the way, Ginny had learned to be a bartender. You could name any letter in the alphabet, and she could tell you an alcoholic beverage and its ingredients. This man had children who adored Ginny, and she treated them as her own. The business sat close to the edge of a two-lane highway with their home only a few yards behind it. As with a significant portion of couples, the use of alcohol causes horrible arguments to follow. Declaring it's just part of life after every story she told me. That also included the night she threw an iron skillet at a patron, and it landed on the roof of a car that was leaving the bar. Or the early Easter Sunday morning when she attacked her man with a broom and, in pursuit of him, had fallen into a muddy ditch, sprained her ankle, and was too swollen to wear high-heeled shoes for weeks. Was this the man of her dreams? Someone needs to tell me how that happens!

Being single and having no children at home gave me ample time to meet lots of people. Blessed indeed to have a few true friends and many acquaintances wherever I roamed. Certain restaurants frequented while on the road were owned by couples who called me their family.

Once, because of a vehicle breakdown, I spent the night at the restaurant owner's home. The home was on 100 acres, with a driveway winding through large Oak trees. They had built this two-story rustic house themselves and were proud of its outcome. Large wooden rocking chairs sat on the front of the porch, and were bright red. Boston ferns hung from the overhang of the roof, and a few well-placed potted plants of Geraniums in clay-colored pots. Their yard had flower beds lined by rocks, obviously taken from a nearby creek. All filled with pine straw and one or two Azalea bushes. Such a peaceful place to live in the midst of Mother Nature. Other than a big yellow cat loudly protesting a meal, nothing but rustling in the leaves from a slight wind.

The next morning, awakened to the smell of bacon, and for the first time in many years, I envied having a family at home. Raising children involved cooking, sometimes even though we were an active bunch, seven days a week.

Often, I wondered if the people who own food establishments cook at home. Well, being that this was on a Sunday morning, yes, these folks did. Perhaps they put on a show with me being an actual guest, but it was a delicious meal. Biscuits with butter spread, bacon, grits, fried eggs, and coffee. And oh my, the neighbor's homemade jelly was delightful. After eating, I retired to the porch. Coffee, one spoon of sugar, in a rocking chair with that big ole yellow cat purring in my lap. I mentioned to my hosts that this was the stuff of dreams: a happy wife and husband living in a forest of blissful commitment. "Heck, I would trade all of this for Tom Cruise," she said. No doubt that movie stars made an impression on her.

By late afternoon, one of their customers had fixed my car. As we drove to the mechanic's shop, next door to the restaurant, things were beginning to be noticeable. When I drive through this town, it's usually on a Saturday.

Eight years later, I still look forward to my visits here. Friendly people get my attention quickly. Today, no one is walking down the plant-lined sidewalks and sitting on benches throughout the town. All the businesses are closed, and the only sign of life is a wayward black dog sitting on a corner. A sudden sense of sadness came over me, and I finally spoke up. "We all need time to rest, I suppose, but I love the energy of this town."

All three of us got out at the shop where my car was. I shook the man's hand who had graciously fixed my car on a weekend and asked how much for his services. "No ma'am, just stay safe and hurry back to see us." I shook the hand with grease-filled lines and said a thank you.

My friends hugged me goodbye, and the husband turned and said, "One day we're going to find you a man so you won't have a reason to leave us."

Waking up the next morning in my own bed felt nice. I sat up and reached over to the pillow beside me and patted it. "Morning, honey, how was your night? Of course, the lump in the blue satin pillowcase didn't answer, so I grabbed it and hugged it ever so gently and returned it to its rightful place. Nostalgia, having been married, filled my head with memories of a man who was no different than the object I had just shown affection to. No words, interaction, or feelings from either, and just the thought of that made me want to get rid of the newly purchased blue pillow. I had given that man so many chances to be what I felt he should be, and after 24 years of pure hell at times, I let him and the horrendous anxiety go.

Papers, more papers, and another year went by. The judge was not impressed when the day came and saw his antics in the courtroom, and promptly told him so. All I had asked for was custody of our children, and I was given that with no conditions attached. The money and social status meant far more to him than the care of a child, and that day showed it when it came to the dissolution of a family.

The new lump remained on my bed, but the urge to dismantle it stayed. After eating breakfast on my back porch, once again, thoughts of the blue pillow became strong. Walking down the hall, I could see it on top of my beautiful comforter, but I had placed the one I slept on under the covers. I grabbed that pillow and almost ran to the guest bedroom and opened the door to the walk-in closet. With one hand, it was thrown, with all my might, toward the back wall. One bounce and it landed on the floor with a thump. I shut the door and knew my anger hadn't subsided, but the added curse words helped. And so, I smiled, half-heartedly, once again.

How does your world end with anger and dismay over simple things? I would often ask myself, knowing the answer was always within reach. If I had been more coherent at times, I would have devised a better plan. Frequently, I laughed out loud and talked to the woman who made me weak enough to endure such a useless person after all. Had it all come down to this, perhaps, if I'm lucky enough, I'll keep laughing to myself.

Chapter 2

Anthony was Ginny's man, as she called him, an ex-military type who had supposedly been a paratrooper during his career. Tony could talk for hours about being in an inevitable war and how that alone had made him patriotic. He was pretty knowledgeable in the ways of a soldier. Tony owned a lot of military-type gear and had a story to go with each piece. He wore some camouflage that made him look important anyway. A wall in their living room held shelves of medals proudly displayed, with more stories to come. American and Army flags were amongst these treasured mementos, and one was outside on a flagpole. Years before I met him and Ginny, he had gone through chemotherapy for cancer. At 5 feet, 7 inches, and weighing 140 pounds, Tony was still a spitfire of a man. Down the line, he had developed a drinking habit that by early evening consumed his whole demeanor. After the nightly bonfire had burned its last spark, that frail human often passed out from the whiskey consumption. Amazing how much alcohol can go into one person and not kill them. The few times we discussed his adult beverage of choice; he would always say that nightmares were relieved by his favorite drink. Who could argue with him? I had not fought his wars. Tony was Catholic, and for him, whatever he did was forgiven the second he asked his savior. Too many times, I had witnessed his heart of gold in helping others.

Tony and Ginny were an unstoppable force when fighting. Four out of seven days a week of screaming insinuations and immense foul language that would end as soon as the alcohol would put him to sleep on the couch. Ginny would call me the next day, and her first words were always, "Well, your friend acted like a fool again last night, but I love that son of a bitch."

Their friends and neighbors didn't seem to mind the shenanigans. In the beginning, I had wondered why. One afternoon, while sitting on their porch in a chair, I witnessed another family in turmoil over a dog that had stolen a piece of chicken off the barbecue grill. This couple lived a few yards away, and as I stood up to get a better view of what was going on, the tall blonde woman swung, and her boyfriend cleared the porch railing and landed on the ground. In the squabble, the barbecue grill turned over, and the dog ran to get the remaining chicken.

Having friends who led different lives from mine was quite adventurous at times. Many nights, I lay awake in bed and reminisced about events at their homes. Laughing out loud to myself, I was always glad I had lived through another fun time. Bonfires and good food at their house were always a treat for me.

Tony and Ginny loved giving gifts that they purchased at local estate sales or flea markets. To this day, some of my prized possessions came from them. Saturday was meant for these ventures, and, having tagged along a few times, I had added to my collection of old clocks, antique chairs, and schoolbooks older than myself. You would think that, having moved quite a bit in my adult life, I had long since given up on more junk, but that wasn't the case. Never having cared for expensive things, I found that items loved or cherished by someone else felt more at home in my life. Being a very sentimental person makes me this way. I still have the only toy doll I received for Christmas as a child. Millions of miles traveled with this beautiful baby, with her blonde hair and pink dress, always being carefully packed once again. And my doll is the first thing unpacked when I arrive at my new abode. Somehow, this one item of pleasure is the only thing that brings a smile from my childhood. And now I could pick and choose people and objects that remain in my life. Seeking happiness was all I wanted out of life now, and a few friends to share it with.

Moving back to the Southern states had changed my eating habits. Over 20 years ago, I decided that meat was not a necessity in my diet. The customary deep south meals are full of fried foods and fresh vegetables. The most wonderful menu for me is peas, okra, red tomato, butterbeans, cornbread, and a raw white onion. And of course, if you can add homemade bread and butter pickles, that's mouth-watering to me.

Summers are the time to enjoy family reunions, friends, and barbecues. One delight is a yellow, meaty watermelon, but I will eat a red one with salt. Gaining weight is a pleasure this time of year, and that is no longer a worry at my age. Besides, I'm not shopping for a man anymore, and isn't that why women try to stay slim and trim?

No worries here, after being far too underweight when my children were growing up. The extra 10 pounds wasn't too much, as Summer was ending.

The season was getting shorter, and a hint of Fall was in the morning air. The heat had been intense the last few months, and everyone was looking forward to cooler weather. Local schools were preparing for homecoming activities, and football games where about which team would win. A tradition seemingly passed down through the generations, which the whole family looks forward to. Even the bonfires at Ginny's house were more enjoyable, especially since you could tolerate the heat. Hot chocolate with a marshmallow on top was just what I needed. Tony often teased me about not being old enough to drink coffee, and I laughed at his antics since I was actually older than he. Unless the weather was cold, Ginny only drank a warm beverage with breakfast.

The talk around the fire that night was light-hearted, and for a delightful change, the hosts had enjoyed each other's company as well. We all had our preferred seating around the fire, and my old chair really needed replacing. Ginny mentioned an old rocking chair that she had purchased at a yard sale and told me to look at one on the back porch and see if I liked it. As soon as I saw this piece of furniture, I knew it would be mine soon. Picking the chair up was a struggle, but I finally made it back to my friends. "So, you like it?" Ginny said. Giving the chair a try and a big "yes!" sealed the deal. Painted in a zebra pattern, the chair was perfect for my home, and I would have to find another chair to sit by the fire. She was always so generous and never wanted money in exchange. Their property, with a few storage buildings, was like shopping at a flea market, but no money was ever needed. My love for old things was just what made me happy. A growing item at my home was anything Asian, whether it was vases or art. The week before, I had added several pieces, but they were still in boxes. Friends are amazing, and I'm certainly thankful for these two.

Though Ginny and Tony no longer share a bed, or so they say, I try to remember what it's like to have someone who would happily want you. Never thinking I would get older without having a significant other just wasn't on my list. My life was pleasant, content, and no one was around to make that any different. Why, at my age, would I change that?

Driving down the street, neighbors were out in their yards, raking up the newly fallen leaves. It's always fun to watch children playing in the yard's pile of leaves. It seems like a fruitless effort to the adults, but it's fun for the kids this time of year.

It makes me think of how gracious a neighbor was to use his riding mower on my yard. His kindness made me feel seen and appreciated, especially since he often helped other neighbors as well. What a great person he was to take care of what little grass I had, because the large trees did not allow much to grow under them. I do enjoy having a beautiful yard, but alas, there is always work to be done.

Many times, I have considered renting an apartment instead of buying a home to resolve this situation altogether. Trying that once, now knowing it was not the ideal place for a writer. I rented a condominium from a friend while remodeling a home, and what a disaster that was! The constant noise of parents yelling at their children well into the night made me feel overwhelmed. Fights among other dwellers were common, and law enforcement was often there, which made me feel frustrated and shaken.

I've long since had the habit of writing in the middle of the night; I couldn't sleep, and with those arrangements, far too many distractions to concentrate. Having your own home meant never having to worry about a parking space, either, which is excellent for bringing in a few groceries. These small comforts make a significant difference in my daily routine and mental well-being.

My world is becoming smaller as I get older, and my patience is usually at a daily low by the end of the day. But with people come stories and laughter that help me feel connected and, at times, remind me of the importance of community. These interactions help me regain a more positive outlook, making me feel more hopeful and less isolated.

Chapter 3

I arrived at a local venue for a photo shoot and a birthday celebration. A large crowd had come to celebrate 80 years of being on Earth for a young-at-heart lady. I had admired her personal story and the hardships she had endured that made her a great businesswoman. Her home itself could be the cover story of a magazine, and the venue today was not far from there.

Azaleas adorned the property of her own Antebellum-designed home. I had heard her exclaim a few times that such a place was too much to care for, but having a great staff was a blessing. The few times I visited there, a favorite spot of mine was a hanging swing in the front yard, under an old tree. A nap in that swing would have been wonderful, and I often thought of asking her if that was a possibility. Wide enough to lie down on, and a pillow would have been nice too.

Wondering why a venue had been chosen, instead of her own property, was puzzling. And later, I heard her say that repairs to the front porch were underway after a recent storm. The same unexpected weather had done slight damage to my place as well, but nothing extensive. Living in the South, one can expect such events to occur at a moment's notice and usually happen at night. Then, in the morning, you evaluate structures first, followed by any property mishaps.

Having good insurance is a must, and every time you realize that paying that high premium monthly is not such a bad idea after all. I'm not wealthy, and I cannot begin to imagine what someone's insurance would cost if needed to repair or replace a structure as large as a Civil War mansion. My small and humble abode suited me fine with the income I had. Dreaming of a large home overlooking the ocean had been on my mind for years. And so I continue to buy lottery tickets in hopes of having a vision for a place to retire.

The property I call home is a serene sanctuary, graced with older trees, including a Bosc pear. The gentle thud of pecans on the tin roof during harvest time, though it may seem disruptive to me while writing, gives reward of great pies. A dense stand of bamboo encloses the back yard, a haven for deer most nights.

The desire for a companion to share a glass of sweet iced tea with often flits through my mind, but a profound sense of peace swiftly replaces it in my solitude.

I'm looking forward to my next trip, where I'll gather photos for an upcoming magazine article and meet new people. Life is magical for now, and I wanted it to remain so. My own historic home is nearly 100 years old, and its previous owners had taken excellent care of it. I feel a deep sense of respect and admiration for the history of this old place.

My next assignment would be among homes that sit on old estates with magnificent grounds. Much like my own, the history of these beauties is rich with many tales of greatness and prosperity.

My house was originally an adequate-sized cottage with a room featuring a cathedral ceiling. It just feels like a place to be, for however long I choose to stay. Initially, it was a 2-story structure, but an unattended stove had set a nearby staircase on fire. Never finding out why the owners never rebuilt the stairs, I accept their absence. It was just another interesting thing about this old place that I have come to live with.

Once I had talked to Ginny about moving to the next town. She desperately wanted to buy my house but needed Tony's approval. He was a tough man to deal with, and so her dream of owning a historical piece of land fell through. After that, any visit from her would be about "her home," and we would laugh at that idea. I would miss my dear friend if I decided moving on was the better idea.

My neighbors would occasionally ask if I was interested in selling, but no one could afford the price needed. Watching the squirrels play in the pecan trees and then gathering the ones on the ground was something new I enjoyed. Working long hours had not afforded me such pleasures, but now was the time for this. Hopefully, my world was slowing down, and the hours were shorter just like the coming season.

As I drove around between the many homes and mobile home trailers in Ginny and Tony's neighborhood, several people waved a warm hello. Over the last year, I have become a weekly fixture here. Everyone seemed friendly to me and often invited me to eat at their home, but I had never accepted. All I was looking forward to was peace, at my friends, in my usual spot beside the fire, and with a few of their closest neighbors.

Most of the housing is rentals for lower-income people. A wide variety of families live here, and some have lived here for many years. I've also watched as one home had many different families move in over the course of one year. Moving trucks were a common sight on the weekend, and it was interesting to see what the next people would bring to the small community.

Having met Ginny and Tony through a family member, they had become my reason to escape a mundane weekend at home.

Local bands offer us great talent many nights a week, and at a few festivals during the year. They are a lot of fun and have entertained us, and I'm so glad many have become my close friends over the years. Social media has allowed me to stay in touch with many musicians from the town I would call home for a few years while working there. I have watched as females become madly in love with a band member. I don't have that kind of bravery, since most are on the road year-round. How do you have a home life and raise children? A secure woman, waiting at home, would be my guess. Alas, that has never been me with my constant insecurity.

Somehow, a relationship had not been a part of my life in a very long time. Ginny's constant words of encouragement kept running through my head, and she was adamant that I needed a boyfriend. Could I do this? How do you even meet someone who would give off a spark of anything romantic? Yes, many had tried, or so I'm told. Being blind to certain things was always a good excuse, I would say. An intimate relationship is rare for me, and those have been few and far between over the past decade. Poor guy, I would say to myself the next day. I told him not to bring a change of clothes. Oh, Ginny, maybe the next one.

The breeze around the warmth was pleasant, but a chill on my arms had made me move my chair several times. I'll have to place a sweatshirt or a blanket in my car tomorrow. These were nights I enjoyed, and the laughs of others were always so pleasant here. Tonight's specialty was hot dogs placed on a wire coat hanger and held in the fire. Everyone contributed to the trimmings and whatever they wanted to bring for dessert. Favorites are marshmallows roasted with a crisp outer layer. And then homemade cakes or pies were usually a good idea. As long as no rain prevailed, adults, children, dogs, and a couple of stray cats all enjoyed the ritual.

Tonight, I noticed Tony giving Ginny a quick kiss on the lips. Knowing them for several years now, this was the first of any affection I had witnessed between them. Highly unusual indeed, and so I jokingly said, "That's a good way to make babies". Laughing was heard all over the compound, and so a running joke had begun: "Ginny was pregnant".

Tony had children from a previous marriage, but she did not. It was something we had never talked about, but I assumed at the time that she was unable to. Being a mother was something I cherished, but it was not for everyone. My ex-husband was one of them, and I had finally come to understand that. You cannot expect people to be parents even if they have children of their own.

If I had known then what I know now, I would never have made a joke about Ginny being pregnant. Sometimes, regrets about words come much later, and for that, I will always be sorry.

Activities around their firepit and food area were winding down; only two neighbors remained. A tall, darker-skinned man walked by us and spoke. Tony asked him if he wanted a cup of coffee and got a yes reply. He had an accent, but I wasn't sure where it came from. The gentleman never spoke again, but finished his hot drink and walked away toward a large white house down the driveway.

Chapter 4

The morning sunlight came through a small slit between my bedroom curtains. I turned over and pulled the blanket over me, thinking that the second glass of wine last night had allowed me to rest well. Rarely do I sleep all night, but it was certainly needed.

Sweats, baseball cap, lipstick, and I'm off to see what local restaurant is open. "Coffee, one sugar and no cream, please," I told the waitress. Most of the regulars were waiting on their food, and a few had spoken when I came in the door. The owners were always behind the counter. My favorite place for an early meal is frequented by many. The hustle and bustle of families, talking about their Sunday plans afterwards. I've always preferred locally owned establishments. Fast food restaurants are a necessity, but at times, you need a place where you can sit.

The large round tables are great for larger groups, and booths are perfect for 2-4 patrons. I'm a regular, so the waitress knows my favorite spot.

There is a square table in the back of the room near the kitchen, out of the way of traffic. A new waitress took my coffee order and quietly walked away. She was younger than the others who worked here, but certainly not very friendly. A few weeks ago, I overheard one of the owners say they needed help and asked if I was interested in taking on a second job. Smiling, instead of a reply, was sufficient for him as he handed me an apron. "I'm not Supergirl like the others here." The cook yelled through the open kitchen window, loudly telling the owner that I could have his job.

And then there he was, the same gentleman that Tony had offered a cup of coffee to, standing in the entryway of a restaurant full of people, but he was very noticeable. Tall, dark, and incredibly handsome. His taste in clothing indicated he wasn't from this town. Dark pants and a matching shirt appeared to be tailor-made for him.

A cashmere scarf hung from his neck with a gold emblem on it. He stood out, like a breath of cool fresh air in the morning breeze.

He was a rare sight, a vision I had dreamed of and only seen in a movie once. Those Italian-made leather shoes, worn without socks, were appealing to me. Waves of black hair, combed back in a style that could make him a model. I looked around the room to see if anyone else had noticed him as well. Not a person who would be out of place in a large town, but here, he was.

Blushing, I held my head down as if busy eating breakfast. The hostess led him to a booth not far from me, and I tried not to stare. Looking so different from how he had last night, I had wondered if it was his brother who had quietly drunk coffee with us the night before. He had not spoken but a few words, but I had noticed his accent was not local.

Sitting by myself, it was hard to glance his way ever so slightly, but I tried. Intriguing he was, and lonely I was. Finally, my hand made a motion of hello to him, hoping it was the same guy from last night at Ginny's. Nodding his head and including a big smile as he stood, walking toward me. "Hello again," he said with a definite foreign accent. Motioning toward the vacant chair at my table, I asked him to sit.

"We meet again; I am Samuele." Not many times in my life had I been too shy to speak, but here I am. "It's ok, I don't bite like my cousin's dog," he said, laughing. Our waitress came and took his order, fascinated by this intriguing creature. "Do you have a name as well?" "Of course, but it's not as poetic as yours, sir," I replied. How am I going to carry on a conversation with a man without blushing when the words are running through my head?

Samuele carried most of the conversation, and I could only watch his expressions and hand gestures as he spoke. Living with a distant relative, looking for work after his job had come to an end in another state. His mother was Italian, but his father had been American and had died when he was very young.

The breakfast crowd had left without notice from either of us. I had errands to run, but Samuele was such an interesting person. He reached into his pocket and pulled out enough money to cover both meals. Thanking him for such a gesture, we made our way toward the door.

How do you say goodbye to someone who has your full attention and makes the heart flutter? I reached out to shake his hand, and ever so gently, he placed mine in his and kissed it. Over the years, a few men had done the same, and it felt good. We walked to my car, parked toward the rear of the building. "Perhaps I will see you again, maybe at your friends.” It's natural for a person from the South to hug someone, whether saying hello or goodbye. Reaching for him, I did just that, and his cologne was incredibly delicious.

Watching him walk away before I started my car, I shook my head in disbelief over what I had just done. I felt like a teenage girl swooning over a man who could never be interested in me. And then, looking in my rear-view mirror, I realized how awful I had dressed that morning. Not even a hint of lipstick now, and I hoped he had not noticed. Frilly clothing and a lot of makeup had never been my cup of tea, but today, I was embarrassed.

On the way home, I noticed a store was open that sold ladies' clothing. Straightening my baseball cap and putting on fresh lipstick, I went inside. End of Summer Sale on signs inside a room, brightly colored with wallpaper and photos of models on stands that made me think of a modeling assignment as a young teen myself. Something I had been proud of, but being short in stature would never allow me to be a model. "Do you have anything for petite older women?" I spoke. Shopping was not a habit of mine, nor was anything bought other than what I could wear to stand or bend over for long periods.

My car's backseat was full of purchases when I returned home. It was late afternoon by my watch, and a nap was calling my name instead of unloading sacks of clothing I would probably never wear.

Not one sweatshirt, blue jeans, or laced shoes acquired that day, hoping for a difference it might make.

When I woke from my nap, the sun was setting. Reaching out for the sheer curtain and pulling it back just enough to watch a red bird on a bush outside the window. What a beauty it was, and other than a black beak, its feathers were almost crimson in color. Another similar bird landed in a nearby tree, and I could hear him calling to her. Off they both flew, landing on the sidewalk. He seemed very attentive to her, and I was thinking to myself how sweet it all was. Couples, mates, partners, or whatever the terms were for two living things together, even in the feathered world. Children playing nearby sent these two flying off to enjoy the night, and I rolled over in bed.

It had become the hour of the day I hated the most. No one to talk to and ask opinions. "Honey, should I have cut my hair shorter or let it grow out?" All the questions women ask their significant others can be meaningless. Now, I would ask myself these ordinary things and promptly answer like someone with a mental illness, or perhaps it was just appeasing myself. Whatever my life had become was unsettling at times, but did I really want another person to fill that void?

Flipping through TV channels, I came upon a movie that would be considered a chick flick. A marriage gone wrong in a big city setting, and she moves to Italy, and it just seemed perfect. Not many of these did I ever watch to the end, but this was too much like similar things I had been through. The main character was a writer in a seemingly happy marriage, only to come home from an assignment to find her husband had moved out. The letter he left for his wife was on a piano in front of a large window overlooking a river. He had placed it on top of a pile of mail, so she would have to find it. As the wife opened the envelope, I saw the different emotions on her face. Wondering whether it was good news or not, the next second, the letter was visibly flying across the room. The anger pouring from her, mixed with disbelief at what the letter had revealed, would have me award her an Academy Award on the spot. Pausing the movie to catch my breath, I wondered if I should continue this, since I have been through this hell myself before. Pulling facial tissues from the box on my bedside table, I can now proceed. "Ok, Annie, you can do this," I whisper to myself.

Chapter 5

As the clock neared midnight, I had finished the movie chosen out of boredom and loneliness. A few tears had come, but in the end, a happy feeling: the main character and I had survived this thing called life again.

Not sleeping well, my morning was starting slowly on the back porch with a cup of much-needed coffee. A bird chirping in the nearby pecan trees made me think about the pair of red birds from yesterday.

Today was Monday, and no commitments until late in the day. As I walked back in the door, I grabbed a blanket off the old chair that no one ever sat in, but it had become a catch-all in my den.

When I opened the back door of my car later that day, the many bags of items purchased the previous day were still there. I hauled everything to my bedroom and stood there looking at them in wonder at what I would do with them. The urge to call someone in need and say, "Hey, I have clothing for you," was intense. Items were on sale, but I still spent more money than anticipated.

I'm one of the people who have a big old chair in every room of their home, and usually in a corner. My bedroom always has two corners covered, one for dirty clothes and the other for a purse, keys, and a jacket. Oversized upholstered chairs from antique stores were a must in every home I've owned, even when my children were growing up. Having placed my new items on the tallest chair, I no longer wanted to think about the quick decision I made.

An old sweatshirt with the college team's logo from a local town, jeans, tennis shoes, a baseball cap, and a touch of lipstick were my usual choice of attire for shopping. Along with a quick sandwich on the go, I headed out to run errands.

Other than a few quick notes, I have been writing all my articles on a computer for many years now. It's so much easier being a writer these days, but today the local office supply store was on the agenda. Long are the days when my home office had shelves and desk drawers filled with items needed for writing articles. It's nice to see baskets, even a live plant on them now, and decorative items that make this room seem livelier.

The mall parking lot was quite busy for a Monday, but it held the store where I needed to get supplies. Being one of the larger stores here, it takes a considerable time to browse, but I wasn't in a hurry. A long row of sale items is always the first stop. The best deal today was #2 pencils, with that familiar yellow color. Nostalgic feelings of school days brought a gentle warmth, and a pack of 6 pencils was added to my cart as well. Being a very sentimental person, I knew they would be placed in a vase on a shelf, never to be used. Designs on ink pens, especially in bright colors, a pink-covered notebook, and paperclips all caught my attention.

Ice cream called my name, so I'm finished for today and headed to the checkout counter. The newest place to eat in the mall is an ice cream lover's delight, but I always choose the same kind, and the lady behind the counter knows which makes me happy.

The guest room has more boxes than it should, filled with items of deep sentimental value, like old photographs and keepsakes. How do you get rid of memories? By having a yard sale? Once again, I shut the spare bedroom door and shake my head at that idea.

The rest of this week will be busy, with far less time for personal thinking. Working has always been my saving grace, as it keeps me from thinking about things most women take for granted. Years had passed since needing a constant companion was the most necessary thing. And maybe I thought, at the time, that it was. Many women raise children on their own, and I was one of them. These experiences have left me contemplating what truly brings fulfillment and connection in life.

The struggles in my marriage over the years taught me I could have made better choices, but I had not. Trying so hard in the beginning to make it work was an exhausting battle. The man I married wasn't on the same page, even after 30 years. Bitter divorces leave you questioning your decisions and marveling at how you survived. Total exhaustion becomes inevitable, along with a vow to never repeat the same mistakes.

The movie a few nights ago stirred something within me; I knew it was either loneliness or a longing for connection. Considering both, but desperately trying not to feel human with very female wants. I had laughed at myself a few times over the years, thinking I was more like a man than a woman, with some desires. And then, one night of 'company' would suffice for the current challenge. 'Oh, Annie, stop this nonsense, girl.' Laughing and trying to look out for myself, this was no different.

Days were getting shorter, and unfortunately, nights are longer now. Out-of-town work had kept me out of a relationship as well, the perfect excuse. Behind a desk for 8 hours a day was never my cup of tea, but being a freelance journalist, chasing stories and capturing moments, was ideal. In later years, I even added photography as a bonus, allowing me to document the world around me in a unique way.

My small car was beginning to get more mileage than I wanted, and soon that would be a huge consideration. I'm not much of a shopper, and car searching is an all-day event for me. It rates right up there with going to the dentist, or any other chore that you wish didn't have to be taken care of. I hear my friends talking about ordering things online these days, and even a company that will bring your vehicle of choice for you to try before you purchase. Not a bad idea, but I'm certainly set in my ways of being old-fashioned. But there's a comfort in the familiar routine that I find reassuring.

Ginny had left a voicemail that said only, "Where are you?" I didn't return her call, but made my way toward a place I had begun to call my refuge. Almost close to her home, the rain came. By the time I reached their driveway, it was dark, but most homes had lights on outside as I made my way down the long drive. Country living was something I wasn't sure this city girl could get accustomed to, but it was intriguing. I tremendously enjoyed my friend's hospitality, and a new sense of family had formed.

Tony stood on the porch, and through the windshield, I could see him waving at me to come inside. I parked close enough not to get soaked, but Ginny was waiting with a dry towel. No fireside spot tonight, but their home was warm and cozy. The aroma of home cooking was amazing, and I could see a cake baking in the oven. Pouring myself a cup of fresh coffee, I heard an unfamiliar voice coming from the porch as the back door opened.

His clothes were wet from the rain, and I looked out the window to see a vehicle, but didn't see one. Perhaps he had parked on the other side of my car, and I couldn't see it, was my instant thinking. Using the same towel I had dried earlier, the visitor placed it on the dining chair's arm.

"Looks like Ginny is cooking," he added with a smile. "I do love her food, and her cakes are just awesome," I replied. Watching as he walked toward the living room, wondering if this was a new neighbor.

I could hear a guitar, but it didn't sound like anything Tony had played before. Ginny smiled toward the door and explained that she enjoyed that kind of music. Blues is one of my favorite genres as well, and how refreshing this was to the usual country music sounds here.

A yell from Ginny that the food was ready to eat, and both men came into the kitchen. The table was just large enough for the four of us to sit comfortably. An assortment of dinnerware and Ginny's usual collection of plastic glasses from dining at different restaurants. At their home, you serve yourself from the stove top and the counter beside it.

The conversation was fun, and Tony's jokes were always a highlight at gatherings. I noticed the visitor's hair had dried, and it was black in color with a hint of gray on the sides. Being much taller, I could see his eyes while sitting at the table, and they were almost the color of his dark hair. His skin was tanned, and he appeared to be in his mid-40s. I had not paid attention to his appearance when he first came in the door earlier, but now, I found myself enjoying his company more than expected.

"Do you have a name?" I asked him while looking him straight in the eyes. Ginny laughed and insinuated that I had met him before. "My name is Evan," he said. Tony added that he was one of those converted Yankee boys. Feeling a little embarrassed, I held my head down and smiled. "I'm shy too," he said. And with that, he touched my arm, sending a shiver down my spine.

Chapter 6

The dinner was filling, and our quaint bunch was quite enjoyable. Having a new person join our conversation was always interesting, but tonight was different. By the time our meal was over and the kitchen cleaned, the rain had stopped. Tony often sat on the porch to smoke his favorite cigars, so we joined him as well. Ginny had chilled a bottle of wine, and that was the perfect way to end the night of our fun. With a guitar in hand, Evan played softly as the water trickled off the tin roof of the house.

The wine began to take effect, and my senses began to dull. Humming along to a recognizable tune wasn't like me at all. But this evening was relaxed, and the wine had helped. I rarely drank alcohol, even at home, but maybe I needed to because Ginny said I was far too uptight these days. She knew me quite well, and we often confided in each other. We were totally different from one another, and that had never mattered, though many times I had walked away, shaking my head in disbelief.

It was almost midnight, and our hosts announced it was past their bedtime. I stood up and hugged them both, not wanting to leave this gentleman who had inched his chair toward mine in a few hours. The air was cooler now, and I was telling him I really needed to head home when he took my hand in his.

Reminding me of the Italian named Samuele, who had briefly visited their neighborhood, but according to Ginny, had left after a few weeks. I looked at Evan and, smiling, asked him if he was Italian. Thinking to myself, what a shame it had been to let that one get away.

We walked to my car, and he opened the door for me. I didn't want him to leave, but I wasn't sure I wanted him to stay either. "Sit with me for a while," saying in a shy manner. Evan walked around the car quickly and got in on the other side. He reached for my hand once again and placed it on his leg, holding it there.

There was a long silence, and I didn't move at all. Just the thought that I was vulnerable and alone in my car with an incredibly sexy man, whom I barely knew, made me nervous. Evan moved his hand just enough to intertwine his long fingers in mine. A strong hand, beautifully tanned and very warm with his touch. Turning his body more toward mine, I felt a rush of chills up my spine. Not wanting to respond right away, but knowing if this was going to last a little longer, I needed to make a move as well.

Reaching with my other hand, I rubbed his arm, slowly turning toward him to meet his gaze. Those dark eyes glowed in the dim light from the porch and held me captive. His lips were warm and placed on mine just enough to tease. His eyes never closed, fearing it was a dream, mine didn't either. It had been far too long since a passion like this had entered my world, so I urged it not to stop.

The shirt I wore that night was a long-sleeve flannel button-up with a t-shirt underneath. Perfect attire this time of year, since the weather was not cold yet. And then I felt a warm hand inviting itself to where it needed to be, on top of my heart. The sensation made me sigh with eagerness to want more of him.

Suddenly, he stopped and opened his door quickly, getting out of the car. The door closed, and I felt my heart sink. Catching my breath and watching him walk down the driveway into the dark, not knowing what to do or feel. I started the engine, turning on the much-needed defrost, and cried.

As I left, out of curiosity, I looked for him at every home on the long driveway. The last yard held a single-wide mobile home with a large front porch and a white fence. It was well-lit on the outside, with matching white rocking chairs. The yard was well-manicured, and it had caught my eye before. And then, there Evan was, sitting under the porch light in the chair closest to the door. I wanted to stop, but felt like I shouldn't after his abrupt exit. So, I dried the tears and turned onto the highway toward town, alone.

The night was a heavy burden, with sleep eluding me for hours. Morning broke, but it brought with it a wave of sadness, leaving me questioning what I might have done to bring about the events of the previous night. Even after a whole pot of coffee, the answer remained elusive. The weight of self-blame settled on my shoulders, and I found it hard to muster any more acts of selflessness.

Ginny called later in the day and asked if I had scored the night before. She had noticed my car was still sitting in her back driveway long after they had gone to bed. Not wanting to sound too heartbroken, I answered, "Oh, just a little conversation." Thankfully, Ginny, who knows me well, got the idea that I didn't want to talk about it and said no more.

As I tidied up my bedroom, my eyes fell on the clothes I had worn the night before, casually draped over the chair in the corner. I continued my cleaning, only pausing to inspect them after dinner. The flannel shirt, a beloved old favorite for its warmth, was paired with a short-sleeved shirt. Comfort was my constant companion, and it suited me well.

Needing more clothes for a load of laundry, I gathered the items off the chair. Closing my eyes, I could feel Evan's touch again. The strength from his hands, lips, and warmth on my breast had made me melt. Sitting in the chair was something I had rarely done, but now it welcomed me. Smelling his cologne on my shirt let me know he was real, and I hadn't dreamed it all. Standing up, I folded the shirt and put it back on the chair, not ready to wash away his scent. Since I usually don't have much laundry, one load is usually enough.

I really needed to add a few new items to my wardrobe for the upcoming trip. The interviews and photography would be in a more elegant setting, so I was glad that the recent shopping event, where I found some fantastic deals on shirts, pants, and jewelry, happened. The different outfits and matching jewelry took considerable time to come together. Two dresses for a few events and shoes that will no doubt make me regret them the next day due to sore feet. Oh my, "the price of being female," shaking my head.

Loading my luggage and equipment the night before was always a good idea. The new restaurant in town would be ideal for this morning, instead of my preferred fast food.

I love the idea of nice dishes with glassware instead of plastic, which some restaurants use these days. Cloth linens were on the tables here as well, and what a nice touch that was. The owners are not from this town but have retired here. Preferring a small table myself, it doesn't bring notice to the fact that I'm dining alone. While eating, my laptop is usually my faithful companion.

I needed to clear my head this morning, and so I asked the waitress for a strong cup of coffee. Biscuits, grits, and scrambled eggs looked good from the photo on the menu, and a few jars of homemade jelly were already on the table.

Finishing a third cup of coffee, I noticed the dining room was beginning to fill up. The food was as I had ordered, and I was certainly glad that I had chosen here instead of fast food today. With a full stomach and an abundance of hot coffee, I settled back into my car for the long trip ahead.

Getting a later start than anticipated, traffic was heavier than expected. Both sides of the interstate were busy with people driving to their weekend destinations, but for me, it was work. The sun came out brighter after a few hours, and that made things ahead seem better. A beautifully amazing estate was awaiting my presence, and the anticipation of the wedding of the year added an extra layer of excitement to my journey.

Four hours later, I could see high-rise buildings on the horizon. Traffic had been heavy at times, so I was more than ready to arrive. Staying at a hotel with its own unique history and an incredibly appealing advertisement, I couldn't wait to experience it firsthand. Driving under the iron gates, I knew the stay would be pleasant for a few days while here.

The building reminded me of New Orleans, with its ornate ironwork and old brick. Cobblestone walkways lined with flowering bushes and a few large statues with ferns hanging from the awnings completed the picture. A beautifully designed courtyard with a concrete fountain in the middle, and birds scattered about on the ground. How nice it would be to wake up to this, but I couldn't help but feel a twinge of homesickness for my squirrels at home and their chattering.

Chapter 7

I always arrive at the photo shoot location a day early. Getting a feel of the town and situation is the best way to conduct business. After settling into my room, I grabbed my camera and decided on a stroll before the sun went down. The hotel's neighborhood was in the historic section of town, allowing for a walk with plenty of photo opportunities.

The paved sidewalks around the blocks made it perfect for walking, even with so many people scattered about. Cafes with a few tables outside against the background of old brick and music coming from inside a few restaurants. I introduced myself to a young couple sitting on a bench near me and asked if I could shoot a few pics. Rarely in my career have I been turned down at such requests, and these two were delighted at the idea.

I gathered some info from them and continued on my way. I've always said that kind people are worth more than money, and later I would send them copies of the photos with a thank-you card. Until recently, I had classified myself as a street photographer, someone who takes pictures of strangers.

My world is simple, exciting at times, and frustrating. Being yelled at once by a lady who didn't want her photo taken, even though she was in the background. I tried to explain that she was not the subject and that she was welcome to move out of my line of vision. "Do you know who I am?" she spoke loudly enough for all within a mile to hear. "No ma'am, you have no importance to me," in my best no-care voice. The disgruntled lady gathered herself with her friend in tow and briskly walked down the street.

Allowing certain things to roll off my back was a hard thing to do, but I had become quite proud of myself. Having less-than-zero patience these days, I'm trying to do better. I never found out who the rude lady was, or if she was a celebrity. Why individuals act as they do is puzzling, especially in front of others. Thankfully, my grandmother raised me to respect others, with a firm voice and a threat of a paddling.

Saturday morning arrived, and after a restful night, I was ready for the busy day ahead. Sunshine, with no rain in the forecast, will make an ideal setting today. My clients were great to work with, and we have had weekly phone calls and emails for almost a year now. The bride-to-be was their daughter, and although she had not wanted a big wedding, her parents had other thoughts. It was interesting to see the dynamics between the parents and the bride, and I couldn't help but wonder about the conversations they must have had about the wedding.

The wedding ceremonies I had been a part of were small. Being a little nervous about this one, I didn't have coffee this morning. Blueberry muffin and milk from the hotel lobby were just enough for now.

I feel honored to serve this wedding, as the bride had personally chosen me after seeing a few of my photos in a local publication. I've never been good at indoor events, and I had almost given up on ever being pleased with my work. But I persisted, and here I am, ready to capture the beauty of this day.

The big day had arrived, and the place was a beautiful vision in the sunlight. The bride's mother greeted me with grace and charm that reminded me of Grace Kelly, an American actress. I had dressed in a long, but elegant for me, dress that would allow me to shoot from any angle. My jewelry was even fancier than my usual wear, and the shoes I chose were comfortable and shiny gold. Looking in the mirror before leaving the hotel, I saw myself as beautiful and ready to capture the day's enchanting beauty.

The bride's father introduced me to a few people in the wedding party, and we all walked a short trail to the garden. Most of the photos would be taken here, among the elegant fall setting, decorated by a florist who worked closely with the event planning team.

The happy couple appeared down the path with an older lady following behind them. The smiles on everyone's faces made my job so much easier, and with the constant laughter, it was hard to get the wedding party to stay still long enough for the serious photos needed. However, their joy was infectious, filling the air with warmth and happiness. Knowing that a fun day was in store, I had an assortment of poses ready to capture their joy and happiness.

The wedding was beautiful, and the cake was the highlight of the reception. Frosting in white with flowers in the same colors as the bride's bouquet. Ribbons of fall colors hung from each large flower on the cake, and the traditional bride and groom are on the top layer.

The bride's ethereal white gown, a vision of grace and elegance, shimmered in the soft glow of the copper-colored lanterns that adorned the opulent decorations. The strands of lights that intertwined the trees in the garden area added a touch of romance to the scene. The groom's Chestnut brown suit, a perfect complement to his tanned skin and dark hair, reflected the ambient light. The bridesmaids and groomsmen, all dressed in a lighter shade than the groom, carried a single peach-colored rose, and the men wore a matching boutonniere, adding to the enchanting atmosphere.

As the evening unfolded, everyone danced to the tunes of a small jazz ensemble set up just outside the garden, creating a lively, intimate atmosphere filled with joy and celebration. Despite the estate's grandeur, the ceremony and reception were held in the same outdoor space, blending elegance with a relaxed vibe, making the celebration feel personal and warm.

The bouquet was tossed over the young bride's shoulder to all the single ladies. And then the groom unpinned the flower from his lapel and pitched it over his shoulder to an eligible bachelor. All done from the porch of the antebellum home with the guests and attendants standing on the grass, and the lighting was perfect, once again.

It had been a long time since I had thought of my own wedding, but as I moved down the drive to an awaiting limousine for the newlyweds, I remembered the feelings vividly. Birdseed flying through the air, covering everyone in a flurry of tiny particles, sending the blissful couple into their new life together. A tear welled in my eye, but with a smile on my face, I whispered well wishes their way, feeling a deep sense of happiness for the newlyweds.

How blessed I felt to be at this wedding, but it was far from what I had expected. It had been fun, uplifting, inspiring, and magical to witness.

As I was gathering my equipment, the bride's mother asked me what I thought of the wedding. And then, before I could answer, she hugged me. "Do you have a daughter?" she asked. Tears had visibly smeared her eyeliner, and I knew exactly how she felt. We walked, with her arm in mine, up the driveway back to the house. "Yes, I do," was my reply. "The day my daughter married, I thought I was going to have a nervous breakdown," and I started to laugh.

While driving back to my hotel, I noticed that many people were still outside the bars and on the sidewalks near restaurants. Music is a great way to get my attention, so I left my room to walk down the streets.

I felt exhilarated after today's event and wasn't ready to end the day yet. Patrons of all ages were out tonight, but more in front of a building that had been a hardware store at one time, with a bar and live band on weekends. Noticing a few tables with guests from today's wedding, I made my way over to them. The best man grabbed an empty chair nearby, and everyone there treated me as if I were a friend.

One can of beer makes me tipsy, and with that, I'm ready to dance the night away. I recognized the drummer as being in the wedding party, and he had made the day with all his jokes about the couple. Telling stories of how he had grown up being friends with both of them, and what an unlikely pair they were.

Two beers later, and I'm the life of most parties, and with that, my newly made friends were far ahead of me, this night. By 2 am, the band was winding down, and I needed to as well.

"Do they serve coffee here?" I jokingly asked. The drummer, who was now sitting at the table with us, heartily replied, "That's a yes, at the Pancake House."

I walked with two of the girls to the nearest coffee shop, as they were staying at the hotel across the street from mine. The band and another partygoer at our table joined us. It was nice to be able to get coffee any time of the day or night, especially this early in the morning.

Just before the sun rose, the three of us made our way back to our respective hotels. I had forgotten to set my phone's alarm, but I was glad I had asked for a later checkout. It was after lunch when I woke, still wearing the dress from the night before, and laughing made my headache worse. Hot showers are miracle workers, but this dress was a mess with wrinkles and a noticeable coffee stain.

Chapter 8

This could be the next town I move to. It was not incredibly big like Chicago or New York, but I never cared for the busy freeways in such cities. The people here were friendly, and there were a variety of restaurants within walking distance of the historic district.

It all reminded me of New Orleans, one of my favorite places to live. I love the nostalgia of old buildings that were once used for businesses. Large Oak trees with an abundance of Azaleas on most properties looked like a movie set, like Gone with the Wind. It was a lot to think about in the coming months, because I was becoming restless, once again.

Making a quick stop for gas and a snack, I was ready to head home. The drive back was peaceful, even on a Sunday afternoon when there is usually a lot of traffic. My headache had subsided, but I was still eager to sleep in my own bed.

A wreck on the interstate had slowed traffic, delaying my drive home by almost an hour. It was a horrific scene with debris all over the road and a nearby hill. The thought that someone may have lost their life made me shudder, and hopefully that was not the case. Several ambulances, a rescue vehicle, and a fire truck were at the scene. At least two cars were involved, and possibly a truck, from what I could tell. A report about this accident might be on a news source tomorrow, and I would have more information then.

I spend a lot of time on the road traveling, and have been extremely fortunate to have never been involved in an accident. Only a few times have I witnessed one as bad as this one looked, and it was bad indeed. They tell me that flying is safer than driving a car, and I do put in a lot of flight miles, too.

As I turned into my familiar neighborhood, with my car safely parked in the carport, a wave of relief washed over me. The darkness outside only heightened my anticipation of a peaceful night's sleep, undisturbed until at least lunchtime the next day.

The next day, I slept until almost 1 pm. The day was beautiful, and the birds were singing outside my bedroom window, and I grabbed a blanket on the way out the back door to sit on my porch that I had nicknamed "Annie's Island." Wicker furniture, a glider swing, and the zebra-painted rocker were the perfect way to relax. Tropical plants in large clay pots with ferns hanging from the eaves of the porch and windchimes to catch the breeze. Animal print rugs with a soft feel for bare feet, and a few matching pillows in a large wicker basket.

The back side of my house was high off the ground, and so the porch was as well. Nestled in the branches, just right for squirrels and chipmunks to frequently visit, and an offering of empty pecan shells is left daily.

My closest neighbors are usually quiet, so this porch is my favorite place when I'm at home. Being large enough not to get wet when it rains, I have spent many hours writing here. More than once, I've gone to sleep, and the chatter from a furry friend on the railing has startled me awake.

Being a creature of comfort, I also recreated a fake fireplace. A candle with a mirror behind it instead of a real flame, and the mantel held Mardi Gras decorations. Many items in my home and on the porch were gifts from Ginny and Tony. Never being one for traditional furnishings, but decorating with favorite things from travels seemed more my style.

I bought two bird feeders recently at a festival in a neighboring town. Both were wrapped with bamboo and fake ivy, and would be a great addition to my yard. Somehow, the squirrels had opened the container that held bird seed and left a mess down the porch railing. They do love almost anything I put out for them to eat. Once I decorated with ears of corn, and the next day, they were all eaten. Animals are fun to watch, and tolerate my existence, as I do theirs.

My week was busy with writing and editing the wedding photos. Very pleased with the way they had turned out, and you could certainly see in each print what a fun couple they were. The whole weekend had been full of laughter, and meeting new friends is always wonderful.

By Friday, I had completed all the work needed and taken care of some much-needed deep cleaning around the house. Ginny had called to say she wasn't feeling well and hadn't been anywhere all week. So, thinking it would help, I told her to put her shoes on and let's eat Chinese food.

She and Tony met me at our favorite restaurant. Since it was Friday night, the dining hall was already full. Many people came over and spoke to us, and a lady from Ginny's church invited me to their Sunday service. I had never been much of a churchgoer since childhood, but I had attended a few if invited.

And then, out of the blue, Ginny said my boyfriend had asked about me several times this week. Looking puzzled at that idea, and trying to think of the last time I had even been on a date. "You should have called him while you were gone," she said with a huge smile. "Who are you talking about, cause you know I don't have one of those?" as I held my head down.

Nothing else was mentioned about a boyfriend while we ate, but I knew who she was talking about. The last man she had seen me with was while peeping through the curtain, on a rainy night. More than once, I had tried to relive the time in my car with Evan. What did I do wrong, or too much of?

I could still see him on the porch, under the light, and how it was all I could do to keep from turning my car around and going back to him. Far too many thoughts had run through my mind about a man I barely knew. Moving to a new town had been my way of dealing with unwanted things in my life, and this could be a sign. All I wanted from a man was just one night on occasion, not forever.

Tony asked me to come and eat hot dogs with them the next night, and I hesitated. Taking a deep breath, I said yes, and I would bring a desert.

I woke early the next morning to visit a few flea markets and a local pet supply store to buy birdseed. Deciding that the best storage place would have to be inside my house, to keep the squirrel thieves from raiding the bounty.

Once I left the back door open, a chipmunk was exploring my house and jumped across the couch while I was watching TV. Iced tea landed in one direction, and my package of cookies ended up across the room, all while screaming at the top of my lungs! And then the neighbor, hearing me yell, called the cops. How do you explain to law enforcement that it was only a Chipmunk? Or the puddle on the floor that happened during all the excitement, and "no officer, it's not blood," answering with embarrassment.

At least the critters were entertaining. That's far more than I could say about any boyfriend that had ever been in my life.

It was close to 5 pm, and I had forgotten about the promise of dessert to go with hot dogs. Tony loved chocolate-frosted cupcakes; the grocery store would have them. It was a cloudy afternoon, but it was cool outside at almost 6 pm.

As always, people would be around their properties, and I honked my car horn at a few I had met. Being friendly is good in the South. They expect you to be related to them or know almost all the local citizens. I found it best to shake your head and smile if you disagree with anything said or done.

The plastic eating utensils and paper napkins were on a table near the porch, with enough to feed an Army. Such are the ways of women here, being afraid someone will starve to death without large quantities. Sweet tea and beer are always in the coolers, even if they don't cook out.

Tony was in his workshop when I arrived, and Ginny said that he and a neighbor were working on a project. After putting the last of the food and my cupcakes on the tables, I walked to the backyard toward the shop.

It was a building that resembled a charming wooden cottage, one that belonged on a lake somewhere. It sat out in the open, and I could see Tony with a cigarette hanging from his mouth, and someone standing behind tall cedar boards that were leaning against the building.

Chapter 9

Tony was a great woodworker and had built many beautiful things in the last few years. Having cut cedar trees on a friend's property, he had planned the wood, and the grain was beautiful. I admired the planks in rich red hues and wondered what Tony would make of these beauties.

My home was old, with high ceilings and beautifully stained wood. French doors painted white that opened onto the porch let in lots of light, brightening the room. There is a large area of wall between these doors and the highest point of the ceiling, a space that needed something to fill it. I could get Tony to create a design from a piece of wood lying around his shop, and then I could paint it.

"What project are you working on?" I asked. As I walked closer, the figure moved from behind the side of the building, and I could see his face. It was Evan, the mysterious man who had ultimately vanished in the night, who allowed me to let my guard down.

I turned my back away from him, for fear I would say something irrational. "Come eat, Tony, it's getting cold." And with that, I turned around and saw Ginny, who was standing on the back porch listening.

"Did y'all fight?" she gently asked. "I don't know who you are talking about, but if it's that man standing out there, I'm not sure what to say about anything Ginny." I wasn't used to anyone getting into my personal business, but she was one of my dearest friends. Feeling frustrated and still a little tired, I wanted to cry alone somewhere. But oh no, Evan wasn't going to get the best of me after what he had done.

By the time I walked to the front of their yard, a few of their other friends had gathered there. The fire was going, and chairs gathered round with music playing in the distance, from a radio. Tony's hound dog was at the table of food begging, as always, and following anyone who offered a bite.

Out of the corner of my eye, I watched as Evan slipped away down the long driveway into the dark. He had not joined us, but had stayed at the workshop on the back of the property while we were eating. He must have a wife, shuddering at the thought of a million reasons for his actions. Or perhaps he was an undercover spy from another country that was seeking out criminals. Being a writer makes you think of crazy things, especially in certain situations.

As we all had our fill of food and funny stories, Tony pulled out his guitar and began to play, with a pretty young female neighbor singing along. Her voice was deep and very pleasant for a late-night song or two.

It was getting late, and the women helped clear the tables, while the men sat on the porch. Coffee was always available in the kitchen, and I helped myself to a cup and returned to the fire. Most of the guests had gone home, but I still needed someone to talk to.

The last person left, and it was just the three of us now, and the hound dog who needed one more petting before he settled onto the porch. Realizing I had been quieter than usual, Tony said good night, hugged me, and went inside.

"That Evan is a good-looking man," Ginny said. I smiled at her, knowing she never would have said that with a jealous husband like Tony around. "Yes, he is extremely handsome, but I don't understand him."

So, I explained what happened the night we went to my car and how I couldn't understand his sudden reaction or why he left abruptly. Ginny sat there for a while, and finally looked at me and, with a wink, said, " Oh, you know all men are crazy." And then that hearty laugh of hers that made you feel like the world would be okay once more. Or would it? Some things shake you quickly, and this was one.

After everyone left, I talked for over an hour and learned many things about this friend. All of the frustrations she had with boyfriends, and had even thought of becoming a lesbian at one point.

I had told one of her church members that I would be there for the service in the morning. Ginny said to come to their house and ride with them, and so I agreed.

Leaving with the last chocolate cupcake for a midnight snack to head home, my mind was now filled with thoughts about the upcoming service at Ginny and Tony's church.

Smelling the smoke in my hair as the water washed it down the shower, Ginny's words came back to me, and how much enjoyment our fireside chat was. Good to have a friend like her, especially one who is not judgmental.

Sleeping all night was a rare thing for me, but waking the next morning, I felt so much better. The dress from last weekend's wedding would be perfect today, but with different shoes and jewelry.

Pulling up at their house, Evan was sitting on the porch, drinking a cup of coffee. He got up and opened the door for me, and Tony was putting on his jacket. Ginny smiled, coming from the kitchen, and asked if everyone was ready to go.

Getting in the back seat of their four-door truck, Evan sat in the seat beside me, and I wasn't happy. Tony drove, and Ginny talked nonstop like it was the most normal thing in the world for the four of us to be together.

The church, a beautiful old building close to the road, was a sight to behold. Across from it, a large cemetery added a touch of solemnity. Families arrived, children in tow, and the minister and his wife stood at the door to greet all. The stained-glass windows, illuminated by sunlight, painted the walls with colors reminiscent of Christmas. The air was rich with the sound of children's laughter and the scent of incense, enveloping us all.

The four of us sat on the same church pew as Tony guided us to where they usually sit. Evan tried to put his arm around me, and I promptly told him "No."

After the service, we were served an excellent meal by church patrons in the parish hall. The aroma of home-cooked food filled the air, and the sight of the long tables laden with dishes made my stomach rumble. Church members walked by, warmly welcoming us and expressing their hope of seeing us again. Because Evan had sat next to me, people assumed we were married, a notion that I was not particularly thrilled about.

Riding back to Ginny and Tony's house, it was quiet. I was mad and confused about anything Evan had attempted. As soon as we arrived back, I said goodbye and left in my car. Hurt by the fact that no one seemed to understand my feelings, but glad the day was coming to an end, finally.

Crawling under the covers in my big, soft bed, tears came quickly. Why did this upset me? I'm not good at relationships, but this whole ordeal had been cruel in a way that was hard to understand.

Waking from a sound sleep, I had dreamed of an island with long, white beaches. The thought of such solitude was alluring; that was precisely what was needed—no humans, no barking dogs, and certainly no Evan.

Noticing that Ginny had called, but not wanting to talk to her, I didn't call back. A pot of coffee and sitting on my back porch was the best place for me, listening to the night birds making peaceful sounds. Just a big warm blanket, soft Zen music coming from a speaker high in the porch ceiling, along with remembering the dream I had.

Annie's Island has been my refuge more than once. With a desire for a water feature, my next creative idea was born. A pond with a fountain in a small plastic container, a water plant, and voila! The joy of planning and executing such projects is exhilarating, and I eagerly anticipate the final results next year.

My home, with all its charming quirks and the comforting embrace of its old structure, has always been my sanctuary. It exudes a sense of peace and safety, a feeling that others have enjoyed for almost a century.

Having a collection of old magazines has proven to be quite handy. The ones featuring home decor or flower gardening are my favorite, and a bookcase in my bedroom holds these. It was getting too cold to sit outside, so my bedroom was the perfect place to pile up photos while searching for the upcoming addition to my porch.

I could still hear the night birds singing when I returned the magazines to their rightful place. The neighbor's dog barked occasionally, probably at a cat, and it made me wish I were more like them.

Chapter 10

The next morning, there was a knock at my door. My eyes opened to see the sun shining through the curtains, and it was still quite early. A neighbor could be seen through the window, holding a piece of mail. "Good morning," I said when opening the screened door. He was a short, older man who rarely spoke to me. "Your mail was put in my box by mistake," he said and walked away.

Frowning, I closed the door and opened the envelopes at the kitchen counter. They were all junk mail, and I wondered why the unfriendly neighbor couldn't have just thrown them in the trash, as most people would have.

Maybe he did care, but didn't know how to express it. Months went by before I saw him again. Another neighbor told me he was in the hospital for a few weeks, but had finally come home. I went to visit, took him snacks, and thanked him again for delivering my mail. We laughed together, and the feeling of a new friend was good, after all.

Two days later, as I pulled into my driveway, an ambulance was in his yard. A young lady standing outside was crying out in the yard. She told me it was her grandfather, and she came to check on him, but had found him deceased. I didn't even know his name, but he had been kind to me once.

Life is peculiar, but I've always believed in doing the best you can, especially with others. His obituary was simple, with no photo, but I remembered what he looked like, and always would because he was kind to me. I should have asked his granddaughter for her contact information that day, but it didn't occur to me.

Placing a sympathy card in his mailbox, while hoping a family member would see it. A few weeks later, people were at his home, and a large moving truck was there as well. It was sad to see all of his possessions taken away from a house he had lived in since he was a young husband, their first home together. When they all left with the truck, I walked over to his yard and stood there. His house looked empty, as if no one had ever lived there, and that was sad. Picking a flower off his azalea bush and placing it on his front door handle brought back sweet memories. "Goodbye, my friend, I will remember you, I promise."

It was several days before I returned Ginny's call, and she picked up the conversation and continued. "Let's cook some steaks on the grill tonight," she said. "Tony bought some good-looking ribeye and plenty of them."

As I shared about my week and the sad news of my neighbor's passing, Ginny's response was unexpected. "Well, y'all better have me a big ole funeral," she said with a cheerful spirit. Her ability to find humor in any situation was truly inspiring, and I found myself wanting to emulate her coolness.

The aroma of the steaks grilling on the back porch made me hungrier. Baked beans, deviled eggs, potato salad, garlic toast, and a cake with strawberry icing were waiting to be eaten.

Tony brought in the steaks, and we ate as if it were our last meal. We talked about my plans for the addition to my porch. Ginny had some old magazines under a stack of newspapers, and after cleaning the dishes, we pulled them out. A woman who never threw anything away, and I was beginning to be the same.

We looked through what seemed like fifty or more magazines before we came across a photo that would be a perfect design for what was wanted. The best ideas are often complex to achieve when you are not rich, but I manage to do so. It was a process of trial and error, but Ginny's patience and encouragement made me feel proud and motivated to be resourceful.

After a thorough exploration of the magazines, I was content with the few that were chosen. Ginny would have been happier if more had been selected, because she had an abundance. Most of the magazines were over ten years old, but they were still in good condition. Sharing these old magazines made me realize that my own collection needs to be smaller before I move again, a thought that brought a smile to my face, but was certainly doubtful.

No one mentioned Evan during or after our steak meal. For that, I was thankful and just wanted to talk about the pond. I packed the magazines, a piece of cake, and a Japanese statue that Tony had purchased for me all into a box. It was only 10:00, but I wanted to edit an article I was writing before bed.

"Next time, answer your phone, woman," she yelled when I pulled out onto the road. Waving my hand out the window, she knew me well enough to know that might not happen. Our relationship was fun, and neither of us said a cross word.

Instead of working on an article to be published, a movie sounded like a better way to spend the rest of the night. The last one I watched was wonderful, but eye-opening. That was what was needed tonight: a movie with less romance. Yes, and not mushy stuff, and then my head wouldn't hurt while thinking.

Listed as light romance movies, I stumbled upon one that was more or less a comedy. Perfect! I must have fallen asleep not long after the first commercial, because the sound of the morning trash truck woke me up.

The first scene had been hilarious, but the good food from Ginny's made me sleepy. Popcorn spilled on my bed, it made me smile, thinking it was better than the movie itself, and recalling a gentleman who was looking for love in all the wrong places. And also, of a convenience store clerk with orange hair who had his eye on a customer, but never asked her out. His life was boring like mine, and I could relate. Single people often look for the first available, not necessarily the right one. Since this movie put me to sleep pretty quickly and didn't hold my interest, mark it off the list.

Mornings unfold in serene tranquility, at home on Annie's Island. A cup of coffee in hand, often accompanied by a local newspaper. I reserve my writing for the night, preferring to edit in the morning when my head is clear. The allure of this home lies in its tranquil neighborhood. The back porch, perched high off the ground, nestled among the sprawling tree limbs, is a perfect sanctuary.

The third voicemail on my phone caught me off guard. A familiar man's voice, filled with apologies and an innocent plea for help. How did he even get my number? Why was he calling me? Realizing I needed more than just coffee, I made my way to the kitchen. I closed the cabinet door, knowing it was too early for alcohol.

Calling Ginny was the next step, and staying calm was the next step. "Well, good morning sunshine, you up early?" as she answered the phone. "Virginia, did you give someone my phone number?" It had been a long time since I had called her by her given name, but this was warranted.

Hurt and wanting to lash out was my first reaction, but then she replied quickly. "Would I give him your number since you don't even like him?" she asked. Ginny listened to me about the voicemail from Evan and the anger that I felt about it. He needed a ride to a job and was told I could help. But who had told him such a thing?

Ginny's assurance that she was not the one who gave out my number was a relief. However, a face-to-face conversation with her was necessary to ease my feelings about the whole situation. I brewed a fresh pot of coffee and retreated to my island, pondering how to handle this Evan-induced aggravation.

Does he make me angry because of the night in my car, from the beginning? Life had thrown me a curveball with this guy, and it needed to be the end of the game soon.

Chapter 11

Fall, with its breathtaking beauty, never fails to inspire me. I often find myself driving for hours, captivated by the vibrant foliage. I packed a small ice chest with refreshments and set out on a solo journey of self-analysis. I meandered along narrow country roads, my favorite places to discover old homes and quaint towns with buildings steeped in history.

Not living far from the state line, I headed in that direction. Crossing a bridge over a river and seeing the sun shining brightly on the water gave me new ideas. One of my favorite parks is nearby and will be perfect for capturing new photos of boats today. Oak trees with Spanish moss hanging from them and almost touching the ground. The winding road through the campground is narrow, with just enough room to pass a motorhome if necessary. Not many campers this time of year, but a few travelers from other states make it a quiet spot.

Reaching a place to park close to the water's edge with a path to wander down, and a barge can be seen on the river. I hurry quickly to grab my camera because water vessels travel faster than I walk. Often, you can see people on the boats or barges, and they will wave at you. A few times, boat owners have stopped, and we've had a quick chat, which is always a pleasure.

It has been many years since I last sailed on a boat here, but most of my memories are good ones. Family and friends, some of whom have since passed away, and the great adventures we had on weekend trips. Only one trip did I recall being a near tragedy. My now ex-husband almost drowned in a skiing accident. When he fell, the ski rope wrapped around his ankle and pulled him under. A cousin noticed and yelled for the boat driver to stop. It was weeks before he could walk without a limp. And then, when we decided to take an hour trip down the river by boat, we came back to squirrels inside our tents, creating havoc. We were all young back then, with lessons yet to learn.

As I sat on a log down a trail between the trees, a deer with twin fawns —a rare sight —appeared. It's not often that deer cross in front of me without being startled away by a human, but these seemed unafraid. Their youthful spots were a clear sign of their tender age. I carefully raised my camera to capture this unique moment. Perhaps being downwind enough, they hadn't spotted me yet. The feeling of luck was overwhelming when the three bolted away into the swamp at the end of the trail.

Photographing birds is a challenge I often find myself grappling with. The stillness required is a test, especially as I age. Success in this endeavor is rare, but the thrill of the chase keeps me going. Two years ago, a Bald eagle soared into a large tree, and in the excitement, I managed to snap only a few photos. A dear friend of mine is a master of wildlife photography. Her patience and dedication are top-notch, and I have much to learn from her.

The trees are beginning to shed their leaves, creating a mesmerizing glow when the wind sends them sailing through the air. Squirrels are diligently gathering their winter food supply, burying acorns in the soft earth. Turtles bask on logs at the water's edge, unperturbed by the world or my seemingly nonsensical conversations as I photograph them. Their indifference is a testament to their natural behavior, and I find it admirable.

Heading back down the trail to my car, the sun was beginning to set. It was a day that I needed, with no humans and Mother Nature showing out just for me. Sitting in my car, I watched as a young couple got out of their pickup truck. They walked a few feet to a bench where the girl sat down. The man got down on one knee and pulled out a ring. How honored I felt to witness this heartwarming moment. Undoubtedly, she said yes because the smiles were huge on both sides. I eased away in my car, down the road I had come in on, happy at the end of the day.

It is always nice to take breaks away from people. Time alone gives me the chance to think and reflect, rather than react impulsively as I've found myself doing more and more. Perhaps it's because, as a writer, I need this time to let my thoughts and ideas simmer, and happily accept that.

With an unexpected cancellation of a weekend photoshoot, the sudden opportunity for another trek toward the river sparked a wave of excitement. I recently watched a movie about a National Geographic photographer on assignment to photograph bridges. That sounds like a great idea, but there would have to be more back-road travel than I would want to do. There were times in the past when things like that didn't bother me, but then being carefree was a way of life.

Ginny was the only person I could think of who would enjoy an impromptu trip and wander at will. Most of my friends still work full-time and have children at home, with their weekends just as full. Deciding to call her tomorrow, rather than go to her house with my plans, sounded like the best way to do this.

As I turned into my neighborhood, a strange truck pulled into my driveway. Silver in color, it did not have license plates, but it did have the new vehicle sticker on one of the side windows. Stopping at the curb, thinking the truck was turning around, I got out of my car. Tony got out of the truck and said they had been by earlier to show me their new vehicle. And then Ginny rolled down the window and asked me to get inside, and we could all eat dinner together.

Tony chose the steakhouse closest to my neighborhood. The food here is always good, and the excellent service makes it an outstanding choice. And Moscato is the perfect beverage for this fine meal tonight. Thankfully, Tony doesn't drink if we go out to eat, and usually boasts that he has to drive the intoxicated old lady's home. Ginny usually has more than my two glasses of wine, so thank you, Tony, for indulging us, I say, laughing again.

Throughout my adult life, I have been fortunate to have great friends. Some of these have been my protectors when no one else was around, scattered across distant lands, enriching my life with their unique adventures. And then there are those special friends, like Ginny and Tony, who surprise me with their love when least expected.

As we returned to my house, Ginny mentioned a surprise waiting for me at their place. Despite my initial reservations, the thought of a bonfire the next night, with them and me, sparked a sense of needed fun.

Another glass of Moscato on Annie's Island and I was ready for a peaceful night's sleep. It had been a delightful day, filled with countless photos that would be edited in the morning.

Lying in my bed, it was lonely tonight. Holidays are different when you live by yourself, and I have spent more than one alone. Even being at a friend's home is a little awkward, which is why I leave early. The silence of the night amplifies the feeling of being alone, making the holiday season a bittersweet time for me.

By 3 pm, Ginny had called and said the hot dogs would be ready by 5, but to come earlier if I could. It will still give me time to shop at the mall and pick up cupcakes at their bakery. The decorations are always so beautiful this time of year, and they make me happy when I see them. Santa Claus will be there, and a photo with him would be fun!

Chapter 12

The air outside was cooler than when I left home this morning. Ginny mentioned the handmade gift Tony had waiting for me again, and the excitement was growing for sure. I'm sure it will be beautiful! Anything from him is an excellent addition to my home.

As I pulled into their side driveway, a heartwarming sight of children running around, and the fire surrounded by a multitude of people. Others were joyfully shooting fireworks, and even the dog, the one no one claims, was there, fearlessly enjoying the cookout. It was a scene of pure happiness, misfits, strangers, and those among us who do not live an ordinary life that most take for granted. It felt like I was part of something special.

Tony sees me as soon as I get out of my car and motions for me to follow him toward his shop. "Looks like you've done some cleaning back here, Tony," I said, breaking the silence. He didn't say a word, but he opened the shop door, where Evan stood inside, holding a sign. The large piece of wood was cedar, with my name engraved on it.

I struggled to hold back tears as my heart overflowed with gratitude, surprise, and joy. "Evan made that for you," Tony said. The vision of them working outside the shop that afternoon popped into my head. It was hard to speak, but a simple 'thank you' finally found its way out. Evan proudly placed the gift in my arms, and a few tears rolled down my cheeks. Tony shut the door behind him as he walked out of the shop.

"I guess it's my way of saying I'm sorry," Evan said while taking my hand in his. First instincts usually get me in trouble, and it did, again. Turning toward him, I carefully placed a kiss on his lips and felt his warmth pressed firmly on mine. There was no turning back now, as he pulled away and locked the door.

Slowly, he led me to an old couch that Tony had placed in the shop the previous year. The passion was so strong and compelling that it made me lose control. I was ready for more, and Evan knew it. His gentleness made me ache with a hunger never felt with him before. Our emotions were intense. Two souls in need of each other, finding total comfort in our shared desire, finally.

Our bodies, drenched in sweat, were fused, our lips seldom parting. Evan's strength was constant, a relentless wave that seemed to last for eternity until he finally succumbed, resting his head on my shoulder. I ran my fingers through his dark locks, holding him close, afraid to let go.

We caressed and stroked each other, and still wanted more. It was an act of passion that made me want to scream, but I buried my teeth in Evan's shoulder and was spent, for the second time. Two people trembling in the dark with an unexpected connection after all.

It was far into the night when we finally sat up on the couch. Everyone who had come to the cookout had left, and the bonfire had only a few embers left. Looking out the window of Tony's shop, where the darkness consumed us, and not caring if we were the last two here.

The old couch became a place to hear Evan snore lightly against my back, and I was happy. Tears were gone, and that was what my heart needed to heal. Being in his arms was what my body had longed for.

A knock at the door with Tony saying, "It's morning, kids." I opened my eyes to see it was daylight. Turning over into those strong, warm arms that had breathed life into me the night before. "Good morning, my girl," Evan spoke quietly.

We searched for our clothes, which were strewn all over the shop floor, and giggled like two young schoolchildren. You could smell bacon cooking coming from Ginny's kitchen, and I knew she would have coffee made as well. "Let's go eat, I'm pretty sure we are expected this morning," Evan said with that fantastic smile of his.

Scurrying to Ginny's bathroom, I tried to make myself presentable before sitting at the table. A large meal was waiting, and Evan ate as if he were starving. We all laughed at his eagerness, and I commented that he was ravenous about a lot of things.

After spending about an hour at their house, I dropped Evan off at his home, down the driveway, before turning onto the highway. A quick kiss and he was gone, leaving me with a heavy heart filled with confusion, and a mind too tired to contemplate what today would bring. My energy was gone, and sleep would be best now.

Standing in the shower, tears welled up along with the confusion and sadness. For hours, excuses were made not to see Evan again, feeling torn between hope and doubt, until sleep mercifully took over.

After lunch, a knock at my door woke me from a deep sleep. Turning over and covering my head with the blanket in hopes of not hearing anything, until my phone rang. It was Ginny, and she had Evan in the car with her, she said. Stumbling to the door, I certainly wasn't ready for company. Ginny was the only one at the door, and that was a relief.

After a few minutes, Evan came to the door as well, so I got up to let him inside. "Your house is beautiful," he said. And then he explained that he had to take an important phone call before coming inside. Ginny sat in her usual seat in the living room, and Evan sat on the couch. Both were talkative, as if we had been in a longer conversation than we actually were.

"Guess you heard Evan needs a way to his new job?" Ginny asked, her voice casual. "No, but I'm sure you or Tony can provide one," I quickly replied, trying to sound confident. Both explained that he needed someone more reliable and closer to town. My desperation with words did not help, and these feelings were helpless.

This situation was becoming unpleasant, even though I had rarely turned Ginny down for help. Her phone rang, and she took the call on my porch. "Tony needs the truck, so I have to go home," she said with a concerned voice. Expecting Evan and Ginny to leave, I walked to the front door, and when I opened it, there were only two of us there. Turning to look back into the room, Evan was still standing in the living room. "Ginny is leaving," I said to Evan.

"I think he wants to stay and talk to you, because he really needs help," Ginny said to me. Her sudden departure, getting into the vehicle faster than I had ever seen, left me in a state of disbelief. Not many times in our friendship had there been questions asked of her or Tony, but I felt betrayed now. Looking toward my front door, I could see Evan standing there, inside. Obviously, they planned this surprise without my knowledge.

Thinking a pot of coffee would help now, or on the other hand, I could throw this gorgeous man out the door and not worry about this again. Tall, dark, handsome, and those eyes that make you melt instantly are enough to let all my reasoning fade. This creature, sitting at my kitchen table, stares at me as if I were the most beautiful thing in the world. His presence was so captivating that it made me forget about everything else.

I felt a hand on my shoulder while reaching for the can of coffee. "Let me help with this," the voice said behind me. Turning around, my thoughts were to sit down and ignore the rush of feelings. But when his lips met mine, the world was okay, and the need for coffee was gone. I was swept away by a wave of emotions, feeling both vulnerable and exhilarated simultaneously. The weakness from the kiss was all it took to repeat another night like the one in Tony's workshop.

The street light shining in from my bedroom window was just enough to see the glow of his skin next to mine. The muscles in Evan's arms and legs made him look like a god of sorts from a movie. And as I turned with my back to him, once again he held me close. The night crept in without worrying about tomorrow.

Chapter 13

Morning came sooner than I wanted, and the warm shower felt perfect with Evan. He washed my hair, as if it were a daily occurrence, and I couldn't remember anyone ever doing that. The feeling of being taken care of was new to me, but the thought was certainly something this woman could get used to. His gentleness was once again perfect, and thoughts of him living here crossed my mind, making me feel genuinely cared for. Any reservations before about him were gone, and happiness had taken over.

"Let's grab breakfast before taking you home," I suggested as he helped me dry off in the bathroom. We chatted as we dressed and headed to my car. It wasn't often that I got a chance to eat breakfast with someone, so this was a good idea.

Sitting next to him at the restaurant, the feeling of his hand on my leg was wonderful. I placed mine on top of his, as if it were perfectly natural. I'm sure to others we looked like a couple, just having a meal and enjoying each other's company.

Evan had asked me to drop him off at his driveway, and he would call me later. I knew that he lived with his mother, but I had not met her yet. Not knowing whether a phone call or a face-to-face conversation was needed regarding Evan, I drove back home instead of going to Ginny's.

Sitting in my own driveway for a while, I felt lonely. Many times, over the years, a partner would have been nice, even for a little while.

The day was beautiful, and my back porch called me from the time I opened the front door. There is always a bird to hear or watch the acrobatics of a squirrel running to hide an acorn. My resort, Annie's Island, and the one place I have escaped too often, was now different. Grabbing a pillow and blanket from a rocking chair, I lay in the old metal glider and thought about what I really wanted out of my life. Sometimes decisions are hard to make, and tears usually fall. No one wants to admit they are weak, a lot.

With a multitude of photos to edit, I poured my heart and soul into my work over the next few days. This dedication often takes precedence over relationships, and travel is a part of that. Those in my life, be it friends or family, must understand this aspect of me. My world is serene, and this is the only way for me to function, usually.

As someone who doesn't particularly cherish holidays, I find myself staying home more often. Invitations to parties are fun, though I only attend a few. Last year, Tony sent a funny list that made me laugh for days, of all the necessary invitations to celebrate with them. It's a beautiful feeling to be loved, and it's felt deeply with these two friends.

Having worked most of the day on an upcoming article about Fall in the South and the accompanying photos, I finally talked to Ginny. She is always in a good mood and knows how to make me laugh. The only mention of Evan was that he seemed sad because I had not been in touch with him. And with that, I promised to call him in the next few days.

Against my better judgment and in a moment of weakness, I sent a text instead. "Evan, pack enough clothes for two days because we are going on an adventure to a cabin in the woods." He had read the text and only replied, "ok."

It didn't take long to load my car with the necessities of a short trip. The leaves from a neighbor's tree were blowing across my yard as I backed out onto the street, forming a colorful carpet. The excitement of what was to come made me happy in a way that only he could give me.

As I turned off the road, Evan was standing on the steps leading up the hill to a home that no one lived in, his bag beside him. Dressed in tan khaki pants and a brown shirt, he looked like a model. His hair shone in the sunlight, and his charming smile made me want him even more.

Our days together were full of joy, and the nights were nothing short of magical. The charming cabin, nestled deep in the woods down a dirt road, was a picturesque hideaway for lovers. It was a place of tranquility and beauty, where I could spend time alone with Evan, getting to know him better. Having packed enough food and drinks, including a bottle of wine, in an ice chest, we wouldn't go into town to eat while staying there.

The cabin was old and had been in my friend's family for many years. We gathered enough wood for the fireplace inside and lay on a quilt in front of it, talking about life in general. Our legs intertwined, and we shared the only pillow from the bed. We talked about our families, how we both had children who lived far away, and wished that were different. Evan spoke of his daughter and the possibility that he would be a grandfather next Spring. He was eager to find out about my children and how many grandchildren I have as well. So many similarities between us made me feel better about this whole situation.

Evan was great at fixing a meal out of nothing and setting the small table as if it were in a fancy restaurant. He even cleaned the dishes as I sat in front of the fire, watching what seemed like the perfect man. Why had I been so afraid of this in the beginning, and running from him every chance there was?

We melted into each other's warmth, and on Sunday, one final time, on the porch of the cabin, with leaves around us from the wind. It had all been an incredible dream that did not need to end, especially with a goodbye. I could not let him go now, and my world would have to change to keep him, perhaps forever.

I locked the cabin door and saw the beautiful leaves scattered on the porch by the wind. Picking up some bright colored red and orange ones, for keepsakes, there was one in particular that caught my eye. It was a skeleton leaf that had obviously lost its color, and I tried to envision what it must have looked like. "Poor little leaf," I said to

Evan. "It needs a home, like you," and I laughed and kissed him as we loaded the last items into the car.

The journey back home seemed to fly by, and we decided to stop at a cozy Italian restaurant for dinner. Evan took the wheel on the way back to my house, a role I was not used to but found surprisingly comforting. It had been a while since I had felt this kind of connection, and it was starting to feel like a familiar routine, reminiscent of years past, bringing a sense of security and warmth.

As we pulled into my driveway, the unspoken question of Evan's return home after our trip hung in the air. He handed me the keys, and I watched from the porch as he unloaded our luggage. The thought of his staying here filled me with longing. It was a feeling he must have sensed after our beautiful weekend in the woods, surrounded by falling leaves and the cabin that now held our shared memories.

While unpacking my suitcase, I overheard Evan on his phone, and only the words "No, I'm not coming home tonight" were audible. Assuming it was his mother on the phone, I didn't ask questions, but knew he was staying. He unpacked the ice chest and the few remaining food items. Pouring us both a glass of wine, his eyes never left mine, and the excitement rose once again.

It was late into the night when we finally stopped talking while holding each other like two young lovers. The stroke of his leg against mine, and his hand wandering up and down my skin under the warm comforter on my bed.

The thrust from his body made me scream with pleasure, and my hips met his every move. Daylight came, and we were exhausted from the blissful night. Going to sleep on Evan's shoulder was all I wanted and needed on an early Fall morning in the crisp air.

Chapter 14

"Good morning, sleepy head," Evan greeted me, a warm cup of coffee in his hand. His words brought a smile to my face even before I opened my eyes. "I've cooked breakfast for you, and I'm sure you're starving after all that exercise last night," he chuckled. The table was set along with a vase holding a flower he had picked from my yard.

As we ate our meal, I asked him about his upcoming job and if he was looking forward to it. Evan said that Tony, our mutual friend, was the one who had told him about the job and had accompanied him to the interview. He would be on the night crew, which is why he didn't have a ride to the shift. His mother's car was not working, and neither Tony nor Ginny drove at night anymore.

"Would you like to stay here?" I finally said. My house guest didn't reply, but quietly cleaned the kitchen and poured us both another cup of coffee. Finally, he took my hand and spoke gently. "Do you really want me to live here?" Evan asked while holding my hand. I stood up, walked around the table, and then led him back to the bed that was still unmade. That was the only reply needed, and with it, the world stood still again.

We left later, the anticipation of meeting Evan's mother adding a touch of excitement to the air. As we drove to his house, I couldn't help but wonder what she would be like. When we arrived, Evan said he would meet me at Ginny's house in a little while. The feeling of disappointment was there, but I didn't say anything about it.

"Where's your new boyfriend?" Ginny inquired. "I dropped him off at his mother's house, and he'll be here in a minute." She tried to console me, knowing that a cup of coffee and a slice of cake from her kitchen always does the trick. "Well, I guess Evan moved in with you," Tony remarked as he entered the kitchen. It's always amusing how news spreads like wildfire in a small town.

Taking my cake and sitting on their front porch, Ginny soon joined me, but she knew I wasn't in the mood for talking. About an hour later, Evan was walking down the narrow drive toward me. He didn't look happy, and a visible frown marred his face. He leaned against my car, but didn't say a word.

When Tony called out, inviting us to his shop, I motioned for him to go without me. For the first time in days, a sense of loneliness mingled with confusion. Was Evan tired because of our weekend, or was it me? A good night's rest would bring clarity.

Ginny wanted us to stay longer, but the tiredness was creeping in, and that was a good excuse to go home. My warm bed, with Evan in it, and things would be good. After all, his clothes were still at my house from the weekend.

Evan, exhausted, fell asleep soon after we arrived home. I nestled my back against his, feeling the rhythm of his gentle snoring. It filled my heart with a warm glow. This man was now striving to win my heart, and it was working. I should have been afraid, should have questioned the events of the day, but at a loss for words, nothing was done. Tomorrow would bring clarity, so for now Evan would be left to sleep in peace.

Morning came, bringing with it the wonderful smell of coffee. Breakfast was cooking, and music was playing softly. "There's my girl," Evan's eyes glowed when he saw me. "Aren't you in an amazing mood this morning?" I said as he pulled out a chair for me to sit. "I love cooking breakfast for you, can't you tell?" Nothing like having someone cater to you, and that had been few and far between in my life.

Evan excitedly mentioned at breakfast that his job would start the following Monday. There was paperwork at the job site for him to complete, and we decided to attend to it after we took a nap. We slept until lunchtime and then dressed to run errands. The conversation was light, and I didn't want to think about any issues.

I stayed in the car while Evan went in to take care of his paperwork and noticed a few familiar faces from our town. When he came back to the car with a stack of papers, I jokingly asked if he was signing his life away. We could make this relationship work and have something amazing had been my thinking since the first night he stayed with me. Our shared responsibilities were becoming more apparent, and it felt like we were building something together.

We picked up his work uniforms the next day and stopped to buy him a warmer jacket. He would be eating dinner at his new job, so we shopped at the local store on the way home. It had been a long time since I had been to a grocery store with a man and had forgotten how interesting that could be. My diet consists of little to no meat, and this man filled the cart up with several different kinds and everything to go with them to make sandwiches. I teased him about it being enough for two on a picnic, and he said that was an interesting idea during his work break.

The word would definitely be out now about Annie and her new beau, without a doubt. How was I going to handle that? A girl who doesn't date and certainly has no patience for that is embarking on unfamiliar grounds.

Thanksgiving will be coming soon, and Evan said his sister had asked him to her house. He told her that he was bringing someone important. The thought of being with people I had never met made me nervous, and we had not even discussed a relationship yet. The anticipation and nervousness were overwhelming, but the thought of spending time with Evan's family was also exciting. The sister lived several counties away, so we would have to leave early to arrive before lunch. Evan told me stories of them growing up and of all the children running around at her house during holidays. He also said his mother would be there because his sister would pick her up a week early.

Ginny was having her Thanksgiving on the weekend before so that all the neighbors would be there. The few times I had joined them were tremendously fun. The air was filled with the sound of guitar picking and singing, and the warmth of the bonfire was comforting. It was an evening of laughter, good food, and great company.

Evan's job started on a cold, rainy night, and he was well-dressed in warm clothes. It would be hard to sleep without him, but I will be there early to pick him up in the morning.

When my alarm went off, I had barely slept. Anxious to see Evan and hear about how his night went was the only thing on my mind. I sat in the parking lot and listened to music in my car, and dreamed of all the holidays we could have together. Would his family like me? His mother was a massive question in itself.

It was 7 am, and I had been waiting for 30 minutes in my car. The warmth of the vehicle enveloped me, a stark contrast to the cold outside. The smile on Evan's face when he saw that I was there as promised the night before was a sight to behold. My car was warm, and he was cold from working outside. My man, oh yes, MY man...and we went home.

Chapter 15

The first week of Evan's job was tough for me, but I never complained. It was wonderful to have someone to share ideas with for the upcoming articles and the accompanying photos. We even discussed the silly book I might write about us and all the fun we have, and how desperate I was to stay away from him.

Getting to know my new man was a breeze, and he was always open to answering any questions. His daughter, who had called several times, seemed friendly and was looking forward to meeting me. The fact that she had spent many summers with him since her parents' divorce was a heartwarming indication of their close relationship.

Evan's sister had already picked up his mother for the Thanksgiving holiday, and she would be gone for several weeks. On Sunday, we drove out to check on her home, and someone was sitting on the porch.

A lady stood on the porch, holding a baby, and introduced herself, saying this was her son. Our brief, somewhat uncomfortable conversation revealed that Jessica had been staying there for about 6 months and was looking for a house of her own. It was a revelation that intrigued me, as I had never seen or heard of her before, and Evan had certainly not mentioned her.

Evan came out of the back bedroom, carrying a small bag and clothes over his arm, when he returned. I could hear small dogs barking when he shut the door, and he said they were his mother's and Jessica would take care of them. "You never said your mother had a roommate," I promptly said when we got in the car. Evan shrugged his shoulders as if it were a surprise to him as well, but didn't give a reply.

We decided not to visit Ginny and Tony but to go and eat instead. The drive back to town was quieter than usual, so I broke the ice. And Evan's story was that Jessica was actually a cousin who needed help after her divorce. Their family helped her from time to time with this child, who didn't have a father figure in his life. "We all feel a little sorry for them, since Jessica doesn't have much money," Evan said with a genuine look of concern on his face.

By the time we ate and arrived back at my house, Ginny had left several text messages. She saw us leaving the neighborhood and wondered why we hadn't done our regular visit with them. The only excuse I could think of was to say, "I'll call you tomorrow night." Knowing Evan would be at work then, it would be better to talk to Ginny.

Feeling uneasy about the Jessica situation, because I wasn't sure whether to get involved, made me anxious. Knowing there had to be someone who could answer my questions, I hesitated to ask Evan anything more. Was it really my place to feel concerned? Maybe so.

Life had been simple, not having a relationship, and once again, I was having doubts about this one with Evan. We had not discussed being a couple, but other people just assumed we were. It may be time for us to have that conversation, so I know where I stand with him and what he truly thinks of us.

Money wasn't an issue, and he gave me that daily. He promptly gave me his first check when he cashed it. Owning my home and vehicle meant the bills were few, but it was nice to have a man who cared about me. If we ate out, Evan paid the bill, and any food we bought at the grocery store.

We worked together to ensure everything needed was in place at what was becoming "our" home. Evan, with his culinary skills, took charge of the cooking, and we shared laundry responsibilities on his days off, which made me feel grateful and supported in our shared life.

Having cooked a few dishes to take to his sister's house the day before, we were ready to leave early the next morning. It was a beautiful Thanksgiving Day as we left for the drive to meet his family.

The sun was bright, and it seemed warmer outside than on previous days. I was looking forward to meeting his relatives, especially the children Evan had talked about.

Evan's sister had a home situated on a hill, far from the main road. You could see it well, and it was a magnificent place. It almost looked like a cover of a magazine, with all the bright color leaves on the trees lining the driveway. Several vehicles were already there when we arrived, but we managed to park close to the house.

A man and woman came out to help us unload the car, and Evan spoke highly of them both. They were very friendly and welcomed me, which made the anxiety disappear. Children were running in and out of the house and a nearby barn. I could hear cows bellowing and watched as a man emerged from the barn with a large, yellow dog.

Within an hour, more families arrived, and we were all ready to eat. One of the cousins visiting from out of town presented the traditional toast and welcomed everyone, with a special thank you to me for keeping Evan in line. That announcement made everyone laugh, and I felt a little embarrassed when I replied, "You're welcome." Long tables lined the walls of the dining room, and guests sat wherever they could find a place, with a few sittings on the porch. It all reminded me of a family reunion, with dishes of various colors full of food.

Iced tea and coffee are a Southern staple, and sometimes, like with this family, a little something more is added to keep you warm. I listened as Evan's brother-in-law talked about his first attempt at making moonshine and how the law almost caught up with him. And so go the stories of many here, who dare to be the one to get away with making "shine."

While cutting a piece of pecan pie, an older lady approached me. "I'm Earline," she said with a Northern accent. "Evan is my son," she said matter-of-factly. I asked her if she would like to join me on the porch, and as we walked toward the door, I felt as though others were watching us.

We sat side by side on an old metal glider that was just long enough for two people to sit comfortably. And then I realized how much Evan looked like Earline and her daughter. Trying to ease the overwhelming nervousness, small talk quickly took over. What do you say to a woman that you've been waiting to meet, but feel like she doesn't want to meet you?

Evan retreated from the barn with the other guests, a mix of family and friends. As he approached, he noticed I was with his mother. "Are you two conspiring against me?" he said. "Oh no, just the opposite," I replied. Earline questioned him about the new calf the men had gone to inspect in the barn. The baby's mother had passed away while delivering the calf, and now the newborn would have to be bottle-fed. Knowing very little about cows, I honestly felt bad for this little one.

Earline and I did not discuss her son, and although there were far too many people around us that day, it was best that we hadn't. I couldn't shake off the feeling of unease that lingered around Earline. We said our goodbyes and, at the end of the day, headed back down the highway. It had been a nice day, despite feeling uneasy around Evan's mother.

We did not talk about his mother on the way home, but something was beginning to tell me that the two were not close. Everyone today had been truly friendly to me, a stranger who was so grateful for that. Several had invited me back to future family events, including Christmas. That would be a great way to spend another holiday, and perhaps by then I would feel more at ease around a particular person.

Chapter 16

The weeks after Thanksgiving were filled with joy, especially the movie nights out with Evan and a romantic dinner at a nice restaurant. A few times, we had driven out to Ginny and Tony's house for a cookout, and they had reciprocated by bringing pizzas to ours for a movie night. These shared experiences brought us closer and made me appreciate the value of friends.

Earline asked Tony for my phone number, and she called me a few times. Surprisingly, the conversation was enjoyable, and I was beginning to feel better about her. Evan's daughter was mentioned to Earline, and the fact that she calls frequently. It was strange to me that Earline didn't have anything to say about her granddaughter, and also rarely said a word about her own son. Being estranged from my parents, I understood, or at least tried. The pain of not having a close relationship with my parents made me more empathetic towards Earline's situation, even if I didn't fully understand it.

Deciding that things should be different, I promptly got out of the car and followed Evan inside his mother's house on our next trip there. Earline and Jessica were sitting in the living room, watching television. No one spoke to me, and I sat on a couch near the door. When Evan returned to the room, he sat next to me, but there was still no interaction with the two women, leaving me feeling isolated and confused once more.

Evan had retrieved more clothes from the back bedroom, and I could hear the barking dogs again. It seemed like an eternity before we left, and my car door couldn't shut fast enough when we finally did.

"Friendly family you have, Evan, they could at least speak to someone when they come to visit," I said, and fully expected a reply now. Rarely receiving an answer from him about his family, especially his mother, wasn't surprising anymore.

At Tony and Ginny's, the bonfire was always warm, and there were plenty of hot dogs and marshmallows. Their neighbors, from all walks of life, were like an extended family. Fireworks were a regular occurrence, and even the old dog seemed to have as much fun as the children. After what had just happened at Earline's house, I was undoubtedly looking for friendlier people.

"Weekends are for romance in overdrive," I laughed and told Ginny. Her laughter, always a comforting sound, warmed my heart and reminded me of the depth of our relationship. Despite Ginny's health not being as robust as it once was, her laughter was a constant joy. Ginny and Tony's stories of their wild younger days, like the one about the bed with a broken frame, always brought a smile to my face.

Often, I wondered how two people who claim to love each other could fight so much. More times than I could count, an abundance of texts would pour in, sounding as if World War III was going on at their house. At the beginning of our friendship, whatever was on my daily schedule would be put on hold so I could rescue them both. In the last year, I finally learned my lessons, and when I arrived, they were both watching television and laughing.

And so, the saga of Ginny and Tony continued, and it kept me amused to say the least. Evan found them quite funny as well and enjoyed working in Tony's shop while learning that craft. The wooden cedar sign, bearing my name, was proudly hung above the French doors leading to Annie's Island.

Christmas was nearing, and a cousin of Evan's had invited us to her house. I was relieved to hear her say that there would be no gifts for the get-together. It was a weight off my shoulders, especially since I had only met them on Thanksgiving. My own family was rarely at home during holidays, so it was a great relief to receive invitations.

Christmas Eve came, and we had dinner with a few of my friends that I wanted Evan to meet. The restaurant we chose was always festive during the holidays. The lights hanging in the trees outside made it a great place to eat at night, thanks to its numerous large windows. The red tablecloths, small lanterns lit, a perfectly decorated Christmas tree, and Bing Crosby softly singing, all combined to create a magical holiday atmosphere that made this establishment my favorite.

Christmas Day was warmer than usual for this time of year. Evan and I sat on the front porch with our coffee, watching the neighborhood kids ride their new bikes up and down the street. It was a heartwarming sight and a reminder of my own children and new bicycles. It's good to live on a cul-de-sac because the traffic is slow here. One reason I purchased this home was the presence of sidewalks on both sides of the street. The homes in this neighborhood are old, with some dating back over 100 years.

We were looking forward to the Christmas gathering at 5 pm. The night before, after a delightful dinner at our favorite restaurant, Evan and I had exchanged gifts. He surprised me with a beautiful, oversized scarf, and I had gifted him a pair of boots he had been eyeing on our recent shopping trip.

We spent most of the day in bed, wrapped in blankets, and watching our favorite Christmas movies. Evan, being the thoughtful person he is, prepared a tray of snacks for us to enjoy during the first movie. Among the snacks was a small gold box, tied with a red bow. Evan took the box, sat beside me, and opened it. Inside were two rings that certainly surprised me.

Evan gently placed the engagement ring on my finger and handed me the matching band. The set was stunning and fit my style perfectly. He reached out and kissed me, but only said, "For now." I was overwhelmed with emotions, unsure of what to say, but I knew in that moment that I was ready for whatever the future held for us.

Holding each other close, we watched the second movie until it was time to get dressed. It was such a beautiful Christmas Day, and the thought of being with his family tonight was exciting, especially after he had given me a ring.

By 4:30, we arrived at his cousin's house, and the guests were beginning to arrive. The Christmas meal, catered by a local company, was served in a buffet-style setting. Green wreaths with twinkling lights hung from the back porch, and a Christmas tree at the end of the pool added to the holiday decor.

This time, Evan introduced me to several people, his voice filled with excitement, and announced that we were engaged. A few of them admired my ring and extended well-wishes to us both, which brought a sense of relief and happiness.

Just as we chose a table to sit down, Earline walked outside. She looked beautiful in a long, shiny dress that caught the glow of the candles and festive lights overhead. I offered her a seat as she approached our table, but instead, she took my hand and looked at the ring Evan had given me. "Nice ring," was all she said. And with that, my heart sank, once again.

I admit that my first thought was to push her into the swimming pool. But as she walked away, I headed to the bar that was on the other side of the pool. As I downed a glass of Moscato, Evan kept a watch on me from our table. He motioned for me to join him, and a gentleman from where Evan's workplace was sitting with him. Being introduced as his fiancée was lovely, and for the first time, I realized that's what we were.

The night was finally ending, and my "liquid courage" had really kicked in. "I need to set your mother straight and not let her keep ruining our holidays," as the words finally came out. "We need to have this talk tomorrow and come to some conclusion, or not." But I remember saying that before, haven't I? Earline was not going to win, regardless of her rudeness.

Evan gently removed my clothes when we got home, and with an indescribable passion, made me understand how he felt about us. We slept as one, far into the night, and his love was felt, after all.

Chapter 17

Winter was beginning to set in, and by New Year's Day, the temperature had dropped significantly. We spent most of the day at a friend's house who worked with Evan. He and his wife were adding an addition to their home that included a large back porch. Their home sat in the middle of a forest with the driveway winding down through tall pine trees. The setting was beautiful, especially with a lake nearby glistening in the sun.

The couple had several daughters, and the wing addition to the house would be for new bedrooms. They were excited to show me the ideas from the magazines they had chosen, and each room would be different.

The warmth of the fireplace and the aroma of homemade soup and chocolate cake filled the air, creating a cozy atmosphere on this cold day. We all sat around, sharing stories and laughter, and it was a joy to get to know this fun-loving family. Later, their son arrived with his family and a newborn baby. I couldn't wait to hold him and volunteered as soon as I introduced myself. He was a beautiful baby, and the fact that this couple had just adopted him made me want to get to know them more.

The three men worked outside on the new porch all afternoon and would come in from time to time because of the cold. It was a large project, and Evan had a good grasp of carpentry. He was perfect at many things.

Tony would often call and ask for his opinion, and plans for a bigger shop were in the works, with Evan helping on weekends.

On the way home that night, we discussed adding to my home and what that would entail. The idea of a new kitchen with an outside door would be the first thing I would add. Nothing very modern-looking, to stay in line with the present theme of this vintage home, but I had admired photos from one of the magazines the teen girls had shown me earlier today. Evan laughed at my excitement about the possibility of a new kitchen and said, "You don't even cook, I do." He was right, this man had become my personal chef, and with that, there were no complaints.

Thanks to Evan's income, I've been able to slow down my work pace and enjoy more time at home. I'm deeply grateful for his support, which has allowed me to savor the simple joys of life, especially during the slower winter months. I look forward to seeing our relationship grow.

The upcoming colder weather and being home more would allow me time to plan for the new addition soon. There's something comforting about being home during the winter, and I'm looking forward to making it even cozier with a new kitchen. When I first purchased this home, a few remodeling ideas were addressed, and the contractor was great to work with.

The next day, I sketched some ideas on a notepad and decided that a newer kitchen design would be more appealing. The joy of planning these home improvements, with gold and white colors to brighten up this old house, was inspiring. It would be a good excuse to buy new decor for the living room, too.

Taking Evan back and forth to work had been fun, but now the thought of him needing a vehicle of his own had come to mind. The only thing I didn't like was the morning when the roads were icy. Sleet and possibly snow was forecast for the upcoming weeks, which made me leery about driving. Often, while on the road, I would stay an extra day or two in a motel to allow the highways to clear.

Evan had driven my car many times and had spoken of how much he liked it. Finally, one night during a conversation about him and his own vehicle, I asked him if he would prefer a truck to drive if he had one. To my surprise, he admitted he didn't have a driver's license because of a ticket he needed to address. The ticket came from the state he had moved from, and it would be a considerable amount if he paid it. So, I suggested that we go to the highway patrol office and get it taken care of the next day.

The next morning, we got up earlier than usual to get things straightened out so Evan could buy the truck he had been eyeing for months. I sat in the waiting area of the highway patrol office as Evan went to the customer window to obtain the information, he needed to address this situation. When we got back into the car, he said they would notify him of the exact amount and how to pay the ticket. It was a relief to know that Evan was handling the issue, especially with the truck purchase on the line.

We had not been out to Earline's home to retrieve mail in the last week. Dropping him off at her house, I drove on to visit with Ginny. She was genuinely surprised, her eyebrows raised in disbelief, that the driver's license situation had not been resolved sooner. "He seems so responsible, so I have no idea why he's waited so long," I replied, feeling the need to explain.

When Evan got to Ginny's house, I didn't see any mail in his hands. Reflecting on it, I've never seen him with any mail from his mother's mailbox. It's puzzling to me because I receive a lot of mail from my box every week. Maybe he doesn't get any mail, was a thought.

Leaving Ginny's house, I told Evan that he should update his address to mine so that his mail would be sent to him. That didn't seem to make him happy, as he shifted uncomfortably in his seat and muttered something under his breath. But nothing said was any different than that idea.

The weekend arrived, and several times during the week I had suggested that we make a trip to the post office. So, I put a note in my own mailbox asking for a change-of-address card. The next day, I checked my box and found it, so I put it on top of Evan's jacket in hopes that he would update his address.

That night, when we were leaving to eat, I noticed the address card was lying on the bedside table. Obviously, he had looked at the card, but not filled it out as I had thought. In a few days, he would have time to do that, and next week his papers and information would arrive, allowing him to obtain his driver's license finally.

The following week came, and it was no different. I was tired, a little stressed, and also came down with the flu. Evan drove my car back and forth to work most of that week. Being so sick, it was nice to have him home in the daytime. He took it upon himself to buy medicine for me and food that I might eat, and that made my sickness a little easier.

Ginny and Tony dropped off some hot chicken soup at the door, along with a get-well card. They both sent texts daily and tried their best to cheer me up. Two days of fever and chills, and I was still weak by the weekend, so we stayed home instead of our usual jaunts.

When the flu had subsided, Evan drove me to get ice cream, knowing it would help lift my spirits. Not much gets me down, but this was a rough week indeed, and I was ready to be on the go again.

Rarely was an invitation to eat Chinese food passed up, and Tony said he knew I was near death and laughed at me on the phone. Chicken soup and ice cream were the specialties of the week, and things were looking up by Monday.

The weather was cold, with rain forecast all week, and I suggested that Evan use my car once again.

Chapter 18

I no longer felt the need to say anything else to Evan about his personal business; after all, he was a grown man. It was never about trust anyway; he was becoming the man of the "our" house.

We didn't have many friends, but the ones we did have were families with teenage or young adult children. Once in a while, we would meet them for a meal or go to a local theater to see a movie. Often on Saturdays, we would drive out to the country so Evan could work on our friend's home additions. That was always something I looked forward to, as the wife and I shared so much in common.

Visiting Tony and Ginny was always entertaining, and their neighbors were interesting, to say the least. At a particular cookout, the man whose property backed against Tony's shop blurted out that he had been in prison. And then he continued to describe how these hot dogs were far better than any food he had eaten there for twenty years. It took me a while to even speak, but Evan said he knew someone who had been to the same prison.

There had been a few neighbors there who had mentioned being stopped for speeding while intoxicated, but this one was shocking. Evan seemed very interested in this man's story, and he actually pulled his chair closer to the gray-haired old gentleman, who was wearing overalls.

I watched the two of them and wondered about their conversation. The man was always cordial to me and had even given me a rose bush out of his yard, but had left it with Ginny to give to me. Not being judgmental, but he was certainly not the kind of person I was used to being around, so I kept my distance.

After we left that night, I questioned Evan about the man, and he said the man had been involved in an unfortunate incident and had served time in prison. Ginny and Tony never discussed their neighbors, and if they did, it was only in a pleasant manner.

Thankfully, where I live, only the winters are short-lived. The air was still quite cool at night, and an extra blanket was needed on the bed. It was beginning to be warm enough that we could sit on Annie's Island some during the day. All of my potted plants were in one of the spare bedrooms, but I was looking forward to them being back on the porch. Still thinking about the new water feature, we had traveled to a town with small ponds that would fit just perfectly.

Evan was very interested in my ideas, and we searched through more magazines at Ginny's one afternoon. I had finally decided on the plans for my kitchen renovation, and next week would be the best time to buy supplies, since Evan's work week would be shorter.

The new year was starting to be the happiest it had been for me in a long time. There are so many things to look forward to with a man who checked off most of the boxes for me.

Earline kept her distance, and I only encountered Jessica once, at a grocery store. I asked her how house hunting was going, but I didn't get a reply, even though I didn't doubt she heard me.

Turning down work was something I had never done, but now my life was complete, and my weekends were no longer vacant.

Renovation of my new kitchen began, and we worked on it daily. Being involved in the process was terrific, and Evan listened to everything I wanted done without any problems. His friend from work came on a Sunday and worked on the electrical part of the new space. Another one of his co-workers came by and hooked up the plumbing for the sink and icemaker for the new refrigerator.

Tony came by often with his opinions on our project, and Ginny with her funny antics, saying all we needed was an outhouse. The only item not purchased was the new kitchen door leading to the outside, and with that, the project would be complete.

Tony had accumulated quite a few antique doors at flea markets and yard sales. One in particular had caught my eye: a beautiful wooden door with intricate carvings and a stained-glass window at the top. It was the perfect blend of history and charm, and I knew it would be the ideal addition to my new kitchen. The stained glass reminded me that my home had once been a church. It was the perfect door for the space between the kitchen and dining room wall, and all it needed was a fresh coat of paint.

It took several months for everything to come together and for the new door to be in place. The entire room was perfect, and the morning sun streamed through the transom window above the back porch roof. The door from Tony's let the afternoon sun in, lighting up my new island countertop with the gold imprinted in it. The process was not without its challenges, but with Tony's expertise and Evan's dedication, we successfully created a space that was both functional and aesthetically pleasing.

As the renovation neared completion, I couldn't wait to have guests over to enjoy the new space and to brag on Evan's fantastic work. The thought of sharing this special place with loved ones filled me with excitement. Now I could think of many things that needed improvement here, and the pond would be next.

Ginny and Tony were the first to join us for dinner after our renovation. I could see her taking visual notes on things to take care of at her own home. With Evan as our chef, we enjoyed a steak with all the trimmings and Ginny's homemade cake.

As the evening progressed, we all gathered around to listen to Tony and Evan's soulful renditions of old gospel hymns. Ginny, with her unique talent, sang and played a few of her own compositions, which always held a special place in my heart.

As our visit drew to a close, Ginny, with a contented smile, reclined in the chair and dozed off. Her peaceful slumber was a clear sign of her approval of the evening. Her friendship was a beacon of light in my life, a treasure that I cherished dearly.

With the warmer weather here at last, I took an array of photos with my camera. Evan was excellent at escorting me to wedding shoots. Nature photos, which are always my favorite this time of year, are great excuses to get away on the weekends. It was still great to have someone listen to my ideas for an article to accompany the images. We had another chance to stay in the cabin from last fall, and the new flowers and green leaves were a delight to see.

Our life together suited us both, and we frequently discussed the future, envisioning what each of us wanted it to be. His family invited us to dinner at their house, and usually Earline stayed out of sight. Through the grapevine, I did hear that Jessica and her son had moved to a neighboring town. It wasn't the best family-in-laws, but it was what it was, for now.

Whenever we went to visit, I would drop off Evan at his mother's driveway and then continue to Ginny and Evan's house. A few times, he was there for at least two hours, which gave me more time to visit with my friends. There was never a reason to question Evan after he visited Earline. It seemed better if I didn't know any of her shenanigans after the last time.

Easter arrived, and we celebrated the day with friends in the countryside. They had always made us feel like part of their family, and it was a joyous occasion being around the young children. It had been ages since I had hidden Easter eggs, and the weather was perfect for it. The beautiful baskets, brimming with candy and small toys, were a hit with each child, and even their playful dog got his own, which he proudly paraded around for all to see.

Chapter 19

I was finally getting used to Evan working nights, with me picking him up early in the morning. We would usually come home, eat breakfast, and sleep until lunch. The days were getting longer, and the hours were better for me when my work presented itself.

A virus was going around, and after having the flu last fall, staying away from people for a few weeks was best. One morning, while picking Evan up at work, I could tell the moment he got in the car that he was sick. His fever was high when checked at home. He was shivering, and his face was pale, a stark contrast to his usual vibrant self. When I came back from the pharmacy, he was asleep, but his phone was ringing. I picked up his phone and put it on the bedside table, but didn't answer it.

Lunchtime came, and I woke him up with some soup and medication to take. Closing the door, but going back to check on him often. When it was time for him to get ready for work, he asked me to call his boss and tell him that he was sick. The man who answered the phone said that many people were out sick, and one employee was in the hospital.

After talking to the office manager and walking toward the bedroom, I could hear Evan talking on his phone. It must have been a family member because I heard him tell someone that he loved them. His daughter had not called lately, and perhaps it was her.

Later that day, Evan was on the phone again, but quickly hung up, saying it was a wrong number. No reason to question him, because I trusted the man who put this beautiful ring on my hand.

By the second night, the thermometer showed his fever was gone, a moment of relief I can still vividly recall. I prepared a light dinner for us, and we sat at the dining table. His usually darker skin was still pale, but he was feeling much better, and for that I was deeply thankful.

The next morning, I cooked us breakfast and made homemade biscuits. We sat on Annie's Island and had a second cup of coffee, and then went back inside to the kitchen while I cleaned up from our meal. He looked so much better and even laughed at a silly bird on the kitchen windowsill, saying it wanted one of my good biscuits too.

Just as I put Evan's medicine out for him to take, a knock came at the door. Walking out of the kitchen, I could see shadows out of the corner of my eye, but according to the forecast, these weren't clouds going over the house. And then a louder second knock came, and, while turning to say something to Evan, men with weapons in their hands in every window and door could be seen.

I opened the front door, and law enforcement officers were everywhere on my property. The gentleman who had knocked spoke to me and asked if "Evan Lang" was there. "Yes, can I help you?" Then another man standing on the porch handed me a paper and said they had a warrant for his arrest. Shocked, I turned around in the doorway, toward Evan. "That's me," Evan said while coming out the door.

Looking at the paper handed to me, but unable to make out the words, shock set in. One of the officers who had been standing on the sidewalk came up the steps toward Evan and placed handcuffs on him, while telling him that he was under arrest.

I sat down in the rocking chair on my front porch, and that is when I noticed there were at least eight law enforcement vehicles on the street from different agencies. By that time, all the officers from around the back of my home had walked to the front, guns still in their hands.

"He is sick," I blurted out to the officer putting the handcuffs on. "Does he have shoes, ma'am?" he asked bluntly. I walked inside, retrieved a pair of shoes and a sweatshirt, and was allowed to put them on Evan.

Two officers took Evan to a patrol car and loaded him into the back seat. "Someone please tell me what's going on," I begged from the porch—watching them drive away with my fiancé, with streams of tears flowing down my face. Then a gentleman who was not in a uniform but had a badge on his belt approached me. His words sounded mumbled, and nothing was understandable.

Sitting back in the rocking chair, I stared out over all the men who had surrounded my home and taken the most significant part of my life away. The man sat on the bench where Evan had sat just a few moments earlier, then handed me a card. All I remember him saying was to call the city jail by 7 am the following morning.

I'm not sure how long I sat there, but when I finally came to my senses, a neighbor was staring at me from the sidewalk. "What was that all about?" she said. The question could not be answered right now, even if there was one.

I lay on our bed and wept uncontrollably for hours. Being physically and mentally sick and alone was unbearable. Why didn't any of them tell me why Evan was handcuffed and taken, as if he were a criminal? The emotional storm inside me was relentless, and its power overwhelmed me.

Not knowing what to say about the arrest, I didn't call anyone. Earline and I hadn't spoken since Christmas; perhaps his daughter should be notified. However, there was little information to give her at the moment. My phone was left on the kitchen counter before the knock came at the door, and now I was trying to remember where Evan's phone was. One of the officers had searched him after they handcuffed him, and he didn't have any items on him. His jacket and shoes were gone through also before I was allowed to put them on him.

My phone was full of texts and voicemails, but the shock of it all was far too great to do anything but cry. Sitting down in the chair where Evan usually did, I could still see the images of all those guns outside my windows and on my back porch. Was this all a dream? A sick, sick dream?

At 6 am the next morning, I pulled up in front of the jail and walked inside. No one was at the window, and about twenty minutes went by before I saw a deputy come inside. He told me a clerk would be with me shortly and would provide the necessary information.

Finally, the clerk showed up at the window, but trying to get her attention seemed fruitless. The same officer who had spoken to me earlier came in the door and asked if he could help me, as if he had never laid eyes on me before. I handed him the card the man had given me the day before; in the hope it would help. The deputy picked up a phone on a nearby desk and made a call, but I didn't understand what he was saying to whoever he was talking to. The whole process was a maze of confusion, which only added to my frustration.

"Can you please help me?" I asked the deputy again. "What do you need exactly, ma'am?" Feeling extremely aggravated by this point, I told the uncaring officer that my fiancé had been taken to this jail and I was here to take him home. The sense of helplessness was overwhelming, and so was the feeling of being at the mercy of these indifferent officers.

After giving this officer with a bad attitude what little information I had, he promptly told me that Evan was not in their facility. And then the woman behind the window asked if I knew where the sheriff's office was, and I replied, "No, lady, this is the first time I've even been here."

The clerk handed me a business card with the sheriff's office address. By this time, I had been here for over an hour and wanted to scream at the top of my lungs at anyone who would hear my plea. Walking back to my car was overwhelming with a mix of emotions. And after gathering my thoughts, I drove to the address on the business card. Mind you, I have never been to any law enforcement agency, as there has been no need for me to do so in my lifetime. This whole attempt was puzzling, and my hurt was beyond unbelievable.

Chapter 20

When I stepped into the sheriff's office, the attitudes were totally different. Everyone was cordial, and I was offered a cup of coffee. Once again, after approaching a window and explaining my dilemma to the young lady, I asked if she could help me. "Yes, we can," she said so politely. Drying my tears, I sat in a long row of chairs against a wall and waited once more.

A few minutes later, the same girl came out and asked me to step into a room to talk, and I followed her. The next words I heard were, "I'm sorry, he was moved to another facility and never came here." "Where is Evan?" I asked her with my voice slightly elevated than before. And then she offered me a hug and said she would let me know his whereabouts in a few weeks.

Watching this girl who had been so lovely to me walk away, it was as if she walked in slow motion, like something from a movie. And then I rushed out the same door and threw up. Feeling like I was going to faint, I sat down on a short concrete wall. People walked by me, and no one noticed me, the fragile, overwhelmed female in dire straits.

Honestly, I don't remember driving back home. The rain on my windshield, sitting in my driveway, with the sound of the wipers, and I sat there.

This was not the plot of a movie I had watched or any romance novel I could remember reading. As a writer, the words; who, what, when, where, and why had come to my mind like bolts of lightning since the law had taken Evan from my house. I just wanted him home, where he belonged. His medication was still sitting on the table, and our coffee cups were in the sink, unwashed.

Everything I did was in slow motion, and our bed was the only place Evan's scent could be smelled. There seem to be no tears left, just the shell of my body going through motions.

On the third day, I received a call, and since the number wasn't in my phone's contacts, I answered it. "Evan?" blurting out quickly. "No ma'am, this is Officer Daniels with the U.S. Marshal's office," he replied. Then he explained what was going on and the need for him and Officer Hearn to meet with me. It wasn't long before I needed to sit down from feeling weak.

The tears started again, and the words poured out in sentences, with me barely taking a breath. "Please, sir, if you know where he is, just send him home!" Reiterating that Evan had been sick and was still taking medicine, I hoped Officer Daniels would do as I asked. Saying that he was sorry and then asking when they could come to talk to me, I replied. "Can you come to my home tomorrow?" I asked. We agreed on a time, and the call ended.

After preparing a glass of iced tea and settling into the rocking chair on Annie's Island, I left the French doors ajar. The squirrels were in high spirits, basking in the sun and rummaging through the flower bed for their hidden treasures. The gentle tinkling of wind chimes and the occasional squawk of a blue jay in the neighbor's yard created a serene backdrop. For a fleeting moment, I allowed myself to hope that this unsettling episode would soon be a distant memory.

My friends always gave me a heads-up before dropping by, but this time, a knock on the door caught me off guard. The recent events had left me on edge, and the prospect of more trouble made my stomach churn. As I cautiously drew back the curtain, a man in a crisp white shirt and black pants, a badge glinting on his belt. "Not again," I muttered under my breath.

I opened the door, and the man handed me his business card before introducing himself. Asking if we could talk and claiming to be an investigator with the local police department, I walked out onto the porch and sat down. "Please, sir, I'm not sure I can take any more of this," I sheepishly asked. "I'm not here to hurt you, ma'am," and then he called me by my name, as if we were friends.

The investigator was kind while asking what seemed like a million questions. He wrote on papers held on a clipboard, and I answered to the best of my ability. Several times, I asked why Evan was in jail, if that's where he was, and the kind man acted as if he didn't hear those questions. His list was long, but it covered only Evan's whereabouts over the last year.

And then the investigator got very personal, and without even thinking that he was an officer of the law, I told him that some things were none of his business. With that, his attitude toward me suddenly changed. He matter-of-factly told me this was very serious and that I could either answer the questions or face arrest for withholding evidence.

Standing up, I refused to be intimidated and asserted my innocence. As he extended a hand for a shake, I chose to walk away, leaving him to his own devices. The sound of his departing car was my victory bell, and I celebrated by hurling my shoe at the door with all my might.

Going to every room in my home, I shut all the curtains and mini blinds, daring anyone to try to get me to open another door. My patience was gone, and all of my sanity was nearing the end, too. Going inside my walk-in closet, I shut the door and hid under clothes hanging from the rod, and screamed.

Lying on the carpet, I kicked the wall until my foot throbbed, and clothes rained down on me. They were Evan's clothes, and the realization of his absence. I cradled them close, tears streaming down my face, and let sleep take me away.

Darkness had come before I woke, and there were no lights on in the house. Slowly opening my closet door, I reached for the light switch and realized what a mess there was on the floor. Managing a smile, it all looked like the time we had made love in this closet, and our clothes were scattered when we finished.

The morning arrived, and the U.S. Marshals were scheduled to arrive at 1 pm. Far too nervous to eat, but I didn't want to appear weaker than I was, so a few leftovers sufficed for now. While sitting on the couch eating, I could feel a vibration under the cushion. Setting my plate on the coffee table, I raised the cushion, and there it was. Evan's phone was ringing, but I hesitated to pick it up at first. Only once had I touched his phone, and that was to place it on the bedside table after he fell asleep.

Why was it under a couch cushion instead of on the coffee table? The phone continued to vibrate, and so I finally picked it up. There were numerous missed calls on his phone and dozens of text messages, but none held names from a contact list. One by one, I read each message and Evan's replies. And then I looked at the dozens of photos in his phone, from women I didn't know, except one. It was several photos of Jessica, some in lingerie and a few nudes as well.

And then the anger set in, like a building had fallen on me to wake me up. Was I that naive? What in the hell had I stumbled upon? It was my fiancé's phone, not some stranger that I didn't know or trust. And then I realized that this was not the phone Evan used since we had been together. Who did it belong to? But if these women were calling him by name in the texts, then it couldn't belong to someone else.

The phone held texts from three very explicit women. Was this all the women he had dated in the past? Maybe before he had moved to Earline's home and started dating me. Different scenarios went through my head as I reread each one. But why the texts and photos of Jessica? They were related, Evan had said, and his mother's roommate.

And then I could hear another phone ringing, but the sound was turned down very low. Thankfully, it rang long enough for me to find it tucked in an inside pocket of his coveralls that he wore to work.

Chapter 21

Almost afraid to look at the phone Evan used hundreds of times since we had been together, I proceeded. The contents were far worse than those found in the first phone, and 'shocked' is not a strong enough word to describe my reaction. Literally hundreds of nude photos were in his phone with names on them. A few more of Jessica and Evan together, with the words "my heart" on one in particular. I recognized the room they were in; it was Earline's living room, and they were sitting on the same couch I had sat on.

Very rarely in my adult life have I been at a loss for words, and now there weren't enough vulgar words to describe how I felt.

Looking through both phones repeatedly, it was almost time for the U.S. Marshals' office to arrive. I hid the phones in my closet and mentally tried to calm down enough to greet them. I made a pot of coffee and sat at the kitchen table until they arrived, and it was all I could do to walk to the front door once more.

Both officers appeared to be in their forties and were dressed nicely, wearing badges on their belts. Officer Daniels held a box in his hand with a label on its side, and the name Evan Lang was written with a magic marker. The box was placed on the dining table, and then both men showed me their credentials.

I wanted to be so defensive toward these officers, but I needed help, and they might be my last chance. I offered them a chair at the table, but only one would drink my coffee. Laughing at the comments about coffee being too strong was what I needed for now. Officer Daniels opened the box, and it was full of files. Thinking it was other cases from their office, I didn't ask questions.

One by one, the files were placed on the table in front of me, filling half of its top. Jokingly, I asked if we needed to use the floor as well, and they both laughed with me.

Each file held many papers, and as Officer Daniels pulled the first few out, there was Evan's name. I was informed that these papers were not only related to this case but also to others in which Evan was involved. And then Officer Hearn added that I would only be shown the ones concerning the recent arrest.

"I'm not sure what this is all about," I said, looking at both men. "No one has told me anything, except that Evan has been arrested," and then I held my head down in shame. "I've been through a lot the last few days, I hope y'all can understand that," speaking with my head still down.

The first papers shown were his arrest report and all the information about that horrible event. Reading it made me feel like I was hearing about someone from a news report. It didn't sound like my sweet Evan at all. Then Officer Hearn took papers from the following file and placed them in front of me.

I felt my heart racing and the urge to run as far away as I could, while reading the words in front of me. "This has Evan's name on it, but who is this about?" Every single word read was shocking, and I repeatedly reread one paragraph because there was no way any of it could be true.

"After you've reviewed these documents, we can discuss any questions you might have," Officer Daniels said. So, I continued the painstaking process of reading the sickening words, line after line, on each page. After the fifth file, I couldn't take the torture anymore. "I'm sorry, this is all too much for me to grasp." The dismay was overwhelming, and I got up from the table and went into the living room.

The two men allowed me time to gather my wits and then came into the living room. One of them sat in Evan's favorite chair, and I stood there thinking how ironic it was. An officer of the law was sitting in the same place as the very person who was arrested at my home.

Officers Daniels and Hearn encouraged me to ask questions, but if I did, there would be answers that I knew my heart couldn't take. Obviously used to dealing with grief-stricken females, their words were gentle and spoke with concern for me also.

Several items on the pages stuck out as if they were highlighted. Repeating those words, one by one, that once again were apparently written about another man. At any moment, I had the feeling that this was all a nightmare and I would wake up.

If it had not been for the professionalism of these two officers that day, I would never have gotten through this. And for this, I am forever grateful. Considering myself a strong person my whole life, this was no longer the case.

After their visit, I went to my closet to get the two cellphones, but I couldn't stand the thought of reading any more about Evan today. When I turned around, my bed was still unmade from the last few days. Gathering up all the bed linens and stripping the pillow cases, I walked to the back porch and down the stairs to my backyard. Walking all the way to the back of my property, I threw each piece into a pile and set it on fire with a lighter that was on the porch railing.

As the fire grew, sirens could be heard approaching my neighborhood, and I wondered what was happening. Before I could reach my porch, the fire department was at my back gate and said someone had called in an alarm for my house. Turning around to look at the bed linens flaming into the trees, all I replied was, "I'm getting rid of a past life."

I opened the double gates to my backyard, and the firefighters promptly moved the truck closer. Damn, I was about to roast hot dogs before y'all got here, I thought to myself. Watching from Annie's Island as they put out the best fire I've ever made, and then the laughter came uncontrollably. Most of my neighbors had gathered around my yard and were probably talking about how a mental health hospital should be my next home. That nice bottle of unopened whiskey was by far the perfect way to end the night, and it did.

By lunch the next day, a banging sound was coming from my front door. After recent events, the door could fall off its hinges for all I cared, and would not be answered. Turning over in bed made me realize there were no linens on it, and I had slept on the bare mattress. My head was pounding, and I was regretting my night with the bottle of whiskey.

Someone knocked loudly on my bedroom window, and it was Ginny. "If you don't open the door, I'm going to run my car through your house!" Spoken like a true friend, I thought, so I got up and went to the door. "I've been calling you for days, and you won't answer the damn phone," talking loudly.

Ginny always felt at home when she visited, so my kitchen began to smell of food cooking and coffee brewing. She talked without ceasing and mentioned a smoke smell in my neighborhood when she got out of her car.

Her coffee was good, but I wasn't quite ready for food. Ginny paid me very little attention as we ate, and I got up to get the bottle of headache medicine. She mumbled about how I looked like death warmed over, and I began to cry. For the first time in an hour, I had Ginny's attention and didn't know what to say.

"Ginny, I need help. Evan has been arrested," I said through my tears. And then I had to run toward the bathroom because my breakfast didn't stay down. I wet a bath cloth and lay down on the couch, and knew this conversation was going to be tough. She sat on the sofa beside me, gently patted my arm, and gave me time enough to compose myself.

Starting from the beginning, and trying not to skip anything, the task began. Ginny didn't speak but listened intently to what I had to say. The words didn't come easily, but having her here was what was needed the most. Just having someone close to me who might understand and soothe my broken heart. After telling her what I could, Ginny went to the kitchen and asked if there was any alcohol around. "No girl, I drank it all last night," and Ginny looked at me in startled amazement.

Chapter 22

Ginny made us more coffee and sat back in the living room with me. Just having someone to talk to about all of this was a huge relief. Within a few minutes, the questions poured out of my friend, and I had to ask her to slow down. Trying my best to answer and not cry at the same time was very hard.

Ginny's first question was about the first page I read, from the U.S. Marshal's file. "Registered Sex Offender" was typed at the top of the page, with Evan's photo, name, and Social Security number below it. Next, it was written that he had failed to notify the authorities of his current address, which was mine. And according to the paper, that is why he was arrested.

Then, when Ginny asked why he was a registered sex offender, I closed my eyes and said, "Because he raped his neighbor and served twelve years in prison."

"But I remember you telling Tony and me that his neighbor and his family from his last home calls all the time, and y'all talk to them," Ginny spoke with a raised voice.

It was a tough afternoon, answering the questions we both had. We finally sat out on my back porch, and the first thing Ginny said was, "What's been on fire back there?" You could see the corner of my property, the burned tree, and a nearby bush.

So, I told her about how I cleared the bed of everything on it, and the need to destroy the bedding. "Girl, I would have burned the whole damn house down," Ginny said with a huge smile. My friend understood, and I had no doubt she would stand beside me, through fires and all. We had that kind of relationship, and having someone's back is a blessing regardless.

I didn't tell Ginny about finding the two phones belonging to Evan. That was a whole new thing to deal with, and I had no idea what to do about those either. We sat on Annie's Island and reminisced about the first time we were here together, while trying my best to find the missing pieces of my broken heart.

When Tony called, Ginny had to return home. Despite my wish for her to stay longer, she had responsibilities to attend to. As she left, I stood on my front porch, waving goodbye, and the thought of repeating last night's madness crossed my mind.

That night, I stayed in the guest room and kept the door closed to my own bedroom. No one had ever slept in here, and it served as a place for my plants to winter. The room was smaller than the main bedroom, but it had a bathroom. Having painted it a bright yellow made it a cheerful space with a canopy bed of gold brass. White curtains on the windows, and both had stained glass in them, which made it the most jovial room in the house.

My grandmother would not be happy about my bottle of sin, as she had called any alcohol. She had a story to go with it as well as a lesson on what not to do. An uncle and his younger days of wine, women, and song, with my precious grandma blushing at the end of every sentence as she talked about his jail adventure.

Feeling the need to leave my house that afternoon, I finally decided to go shopping. The grocery store seemed quiet for a late afternoon until I turned down the first aisle. There, Jessica stood, her son innocently examining the canned goods. The urge to pick up a can of peaches and hurl it at her was overwhelming, dominating my thoughts.

Going past that aisle, I didn't stop again until the middle of the store, while trying my best to regain my composure. While picking up a loaf of bread, a familiar voice called my name, and a brutal chill went up my spine. It was Earline, with Jessica standing beside the shopping cart. "We need to talk," Earline said rudely. "I have nothing to say to you or Jessica," and then I pushed my cart away and headed for the checkout counters.

After swiftly paying for my items, I marched to my car with determination. As I left the parking lot and chose a different route home, the audacity of their approach fueled my anger. I immediately called Ginny and recounted the incident, and she was equally shocked. While they hadn't made any direct threats, the intimidation was enough to prompt me to seek legal advice later.

The lawyer advised me to sit still and see what happens next. Because I had not been charged in all this, being the innocent victim, there was no need to do anything. He also said to let him know immediately if either of the women reencounters me.

Getting out of town was the best thing I knew to do to save what little sanity I had left. The best place to get lost for me is an island off the coast of Florida. Often, I've called it my peace and have escaped there more than once.

Spending time away, just sitting on the sand, was pure paradise. A small beach house with a porch just big enough for a chair. Only one store with two gas pumps, a small grocery store, and a good restaurant, all in the same building. There had been talks of more houses being built on the island, but the dozen there was all it had for now.

Half of the homes were rentals used only by families during the summer months. The locals were friendly and spoke, but mostly kept to themselves. All in all, it was the perfect place to clear your head, any time of the year. I had spoken to the owner of the one I rented several times about buying this one. He always says it's his retirement income, but his wife enjoys the money more than he does.

I love seashells and collect some on every trip to the island. Many baskets and old glass containers at my home have been filled with this beach's sand, with shells added. Mother Nature has been good to this part of the world, and the sand is a brilliant white. Tiny crabs wandered the dunes at night and scared me a time or two. But I would gladly trade them for the squirrels who wreak havoc in my flower beds back home.

Orange juice and a bagel in hand, the morning is spent thinking about where my life needs to go from here. This is a good place to move to, and I was looking for my next home last year. "You're not getting any younger, Annie," I reminded myself. Being here is truly my Nirvana and blissfully so.

My time on the island ended, and I didn't want to think about what was ahead. I had barely looked at my phone while there, but knew there were a lot of texts and calls waiting for me to reply. The drive back was lovely, and I stopped one more time before the state line at a great seafood restaurant I've eaten at before. They were opening, so it still allowed time to get back home before dark.

Only packing a small suitcase, there was not much to unload when I arrived. Later, going out to check my mailbox, there were two boxes behind the rocking chair on my porch. No packages were expected during my absence, but I took them inside, and there were no names on either box. Opening the bigger box first, I could see shirts that were larger than my own size. The second box contained a note addressed to me. All it said was that the clothes belonged to Evan and were no longer wanted at her house, signed "Jessica."

First of all, how in the hell did she know where I lived? Secondly, why in the world would I want his clothes! Dumping them over the rail on my back porch, a new vision of a fire occurred in my head. Buttttt.... The fire chief had warned me never to do it again, or I would face charges.

Sending a text to Ginny, "bonfire needed with a few things to get rid of." "I assume you are home," Ginny replied. The war was on now, revenge is mine, sayeth Annie!

Most of the texts and missed calls on my phone were junk, and only a couple were worth replying to. The first was from an attorney in a neighboring town, who said he had been appointed to represent Mr. Evan Lang and asked me to contact him immediately. The second text was from Earline, asking for a list of items she said belonged to her son and demanded be brought to her home.

You know, I've spent my life being a good person and telling others they needed to be as well, but I'd become someone full of hate I didn't recognize anymore.

Chapter 23

After calling my attorney about the boxes Jessica had left, I was totally frustrated when I hung up. He was the one who said to notify him of any more confrontations, but now my concerns were not being taken seriously. Promptly telling the attorney that I would send him the boxes, because my fury was rising, and then he could have a bonfire with them, since trash burns well.

On the list of items that Earline wanted from me were the rings that Evan had given me. Why would she want those? After all, they were new when I received them, and now they were back in the box they came in, with the jewelry store's logo. Another strange request was a pair of ladies' boots that belonged to Jessica. Also on the list was a pink ladies' bathrobe belonging to another woman I didn't know. And of course, Earline asked for anything that he had at my house, including his underwear. After I read the list to my now ex-attorney, he laughed and said she was definitely a mental case.

Next on my list was calling the attorney appointed for Evan—the dreaded phone call that took every ounce of strength. His secretary told me that he was in court, but would call me back after lunch. Sighing, I almost turned my cell phone off so that he couldn't call back.

It was 2:00 before Evan's attorney called, and I was scared. After getting off the phone with him, the shock was unbelievable. He answered most of my questions but said he was not at liberty to discuss a few of them. Evan had given him my name, phone number, and address, with the approval to contact me as soon as possible.

Evan had been taken to a prison on the other side of the state, about an hour after they arrested him. He was indeed a registered sex offender, and yes.... everything in the files from the U.S. Marshal's office was true. Evan's prison time was served in another state from which he had moved, and then he relocated to his mother's residence in my town. The attorney said the reason for his arrest was that he had not notified the proper authorities and his probation officer of his move to my home.

How can a man live with you for almost a year, and the thoughts of him now make no sense? I knew absolutely nothing about the person who had consumed my life, day after day. And then there were a million questions I had to ask of myself, being the only one to answer those.

My rocking chair on Annie's Island was the one that Ginny had given me last year. Often, I've called it my thinking chair. Pouring myself a glass of Moscato and walking to its spot, I spoke to this old chair. "Chair, we have a lot of talking to do, and I need you to listen with your ears open wide," speaking to it as I often did.

I'm not sure if I drank more wine or the 900 tears that went into my glass, but me and that old chair rocked for hours. And sometime after dark, I knew what to do.

I called Ginny and told her all the info I have on Evan, as of now. Finally, she told Tony they were coming to my house and to put on his shoes. "We are going to stop for chicken meals, and then we will be right there," Ginny said to me.

I had just enough time to shower before Ginny and Tony arrived, with their abundance of food in tow. We sat at the table and talked about the mess that Evan had created for me. Even though Tony was a strong man, he wiped a few tears from his own face.

The only conclusion we came to was that life is horrible sometimes, but I didn't deserve any of this. Ginny was adamant that I have a reasonable attorney, regardless. She was well acquainted with several state officials and considered a few her friends. Telling me that she would make phone calls in the morning to find the perfect attorney for me was a blessing.

I slept well that night and had more clarity about things, thanks to my dearest friends. The guest room bed suited me well, and the thoughts of moving to my favorite island took me to sleep.

Within a few days, a high-powered attorney from the state capital called me, offering detailed advice and support. He said that a local state representative had contacted him on my behalf. This man was highly knowledgeable about these kinds of affairs and was more helpful than I could have imagined. He gave me a list of things to consider and things that I absolutely did not need to do. And he even gave me his personal cell phone number and said to call or text anytime, day or night, if required.

The representative emphasized that since I had not been charged and was an innocent party, legal representation was not necessary. It helped me understand the advice he and the attorney were giving, and why it was important.

Calling Ginny to tell her about that phone call made me feel so much better. What a doll she was to help anytime I needed it, and if she loved you, that was a given.

By this point, there were so many texts and missed phone calls that I could not keep up. I only stayed in contact with a few people, and that was sparse. My energy was low, and my brain couldn't handle basic chit-chat conversations. Some of those were neighbors who had either witnessed the arrest or the fire trucks with the tree blazing.

I'm one of those low-key people, and only a few know where I live, and most of my neighbors have no idea who I am. Finding that's the best way for me to live, except when 900 law enforcement officers invade your property, or you set half of your yard on fire.

I've laughed at myself because I'm pretty good at being incognito. Enjoying my work as a traveler and not needing to entertain at home, it gives neighbors something to talk about wherever I'm living. Evan had been the same while living with me, especially since he slept during the day and worked at night. Our schedules had worked together in harmony.

During one of our conversations, Ginny suggested that adopting a cat for company might be a great idea. She even said they would come and feed it if I were out of town. Right now, I couldn't even remember to feed myself, much less a pet, but companionship would be nice, one day.

Three weeks after Evan was arrested, I received a phone call, but didn't answer it. Looking up the business name listed and the number, it turned out to be a correctional facility. No voicemail included, so I didn't return the call that day. A few days later, the same number called, and I answered, but it was a recording telling about how to put money on someone's account at that facility.

I called the representative and asked if that was something possible associated with Evan. And yes, it was at the same prison where Evan was held, I was told. Thanking him for the info, he said to please stay in touch.

The thought of talking to someone, anyone, in a prison was incomprehensible and was certainly not how I lived my life. My temper rose, and then the next call, a few minutes later, was from the same correctional facility.

Answering the phone with a forceful "what" instead of "hello" might have been a shock to him, but Evan spoke anyway.

My church upbringing reminds me, as of lately, that ladies don't use four-letter words. Women are supposed to act and speak as if they are educated enough to use proper language, no matter what. Today was NOT that day!

I listened as Evan, the prisoner, asked me to put money on something called 'his books'. And then he told me how much he loved and missed me. Then, it was my turn. Calling him everything but a male human being, and not stopping, my anger continued. And at the end of my short but assertive sentences, he had the nerve to say, "I love you, and will call again soon."

Throwing my phone off the back porch and almost hitting a squirrel in the process, I screamed. As a matter of fact, it was so loud that a neighbor yelled, asking if everything was okay and if help was needed! With that, one of those four-letter words used on Evan today came out. My life was going to hell, in a hand basket, and I screamed again, with more vulgar words.

My grandfather would be ashamed; he had raised me better than this. My ideas had run out, and I was tired of talking period. Who else could I turn to for help?

Chapter 24

For a few weeks, I didn't receive any more calls from Evan. I was so thankful for that, because his call helped me process my feelings and understand the emotional impact. The feeling he didn't care was obvious. He honestly didn't feel like he had done anything wrong, ever. Well, Mr. Lang, I've got news for you!

His call allowed me to vent deep anger and hurt, and with that, it made me stronger and meaner. I did leave a note in the neighbor's mailbox, apologizing and promising to do better, after throwing my phone.

And then, after about 3 weeks, the letters started arriving. It was the same as his phone calls, and they were disgusting to read—no apology, no admission of guilt, and all innocent words of BS. Oh, how he missed me and loved me so much, which made the emotional conflict even more intense, and he couldn't wait to get home, and on and on and on. But the final words were, "Please put money on my books so I can eat." Every single letter was a lie; all lies from start to finish.

After four letters, I finally responded with a new sense of pure hate. Five pages, front and back, with every available space I wrote to Evan. My anger was harsh and to the point. There were no feelings left after finishing, and I took it to the post office instead of mailing it in my own mailbox.

The following letter from Evan came from another facility. He had been moved, and they were taking him to serve more time in another state. He did not elaborate on that, so I have no idea why they moved him. It was very apparent in his letter that he had spoken to his mother. He asked me to please give Earline the items she asked for and to let her know the rings he had given me were actually Jessica's. Then, once again, the same things: I miss you, will be home soon, and signed, I love you, Evan.

That was the last letter, but I did receive a phone call weeks later from a correctional facility in another state. I knew it was him, but nothing else could be said; I was done. The unanswered call marked the end of my emotional journey and the final decision I made about communication with Evan.

While sitting at a bonfire at Ginny and Tony's house, I asked the gentleman that Evan had spoken to last year about their conversation. The man was a little hesitant, but told me they had the same probation officer. My eyes must have gotten as big as saucers while I was listening to how this person had once been in the same prison as Evan. And then he told me the probation officer's name and where to find them. I shook the man's hand and asked Ginny for paper and a pen to write down the info.

Driving to the address the man had given, only to find out it was the sheriff's office, was disappointing. It was the same place I had desperately tried to acquire information after Evan's arrest. Asking the same unfriendly lady at the desk about the person I needed to speak with, she only pointed at a dark green door.

When I opened that door, several people were moving about, but one lady was at a desk on the phone. No one seemed to be interested in helping me, and they just went about their business. The lady finally hung up her phone, and I quickly approached her. At first, she was not any friendlier than the other people who worked there, but then a look on her face changed.

She handed me two facial tissues from her desk and asked me to repeat the name. After asking for my identification, she began to talk.

The tissues came in handy after listening to how many women he had deceived and had already been to this office since his arrest. Women? What women? I kept asking her until she got up and hugged me.

This never-ending nightmare took on another page of horror, and the probation officer kindly helped me to understand. I quietly sat while slowly shaking my head, over and over and over, once more. "How much more can I take?" I asked the officer. "Honey, it will get better, but it may take a while," her words were clear.

I don't remember walking to my car, but my heart was bursting from the pain of Evan Lang.

All week, I worked quietly at home and had taken only a few phone calls. Several friends asked me to go out and eat, but I wasn't sure I'd be much company. With the days warmer, the small pond on Annie's Island was on my mind again. Enclosing this porch was another idea that came to mind, and then the potted plants could be left in it year-round, along with the free-standing pond.

The next morning, I visited a local building supply store and inquired about such a plan, and they had fantastic ideas as well. Desperately needing something to take my mind off the last year, I browsed a local bookstore for magazines on home gardening and a few that specialized in porch renovations.

With a sketch pad in hand, I had my ideas of what would complete Annie's Island and keep me preoccupied for a while, at least. A nearby town always had the most beautiful parks, with fresh flowers planted each year. I read in a local paper that they had just renovated their award-winning park and added new structures.

"Get your shoes on, Ginny girl, we're going looking," I said happily, standing at her door. She didn't hesitate and told Tony we would be back later. We drove over to the park, and it was truly magnificent. I must have taken 200 photos because there was so much to see, and the additions to the grounds were excellent as well.

It had been a long time since a greenhouse had been on any of my properties, and I knew it was a lot of work. The park had added two small ponds, and you could easily replace plants around the outside since they were in flower pots. In all, it was the perfect idea for the pond on my back porch to complete Annie's Island.

Ginny and I filled my car with all the wonderful things I purchased from the park's gift shop and headed home. Going over there and coming back, we didn't talk about anything but my plans for the porch. The excitement was growing with my new project, and Ginny promised to be a great helper.

By next week, I had lined up a contractor to add onto Annie's Island and enclose the whole structure. This porch was going to be everything envisioned and more. The new windows added would open and close, and a few did not have wire screens so that birds and maybe an unruly squirrel could enter.

I sat on my porch, thinking about why it was called "Annie's Island." It brought me peace at a time when I was first moving into this home, and oh, how that was needed. Often telling friends that if a beach were in my backyard, this would be perfect. My new pond would suffice for now and help to heal my spirit.

My contractor and his men were quick to get started, and the noise itself brought excitement. Planting new flowers and trees in my front yard gave me plenty to do, and with the addition of new front porch decor, it was stunning. A few neighbors had stopped to talk about how beautiful it all was, and that was nice to hear after the turmoil I had caused there.

The thoughts were constant: nothing more than to get on with my life and be happy once more. The sun was beginning to darken my skin, and I didn't look like the kiss of death was around me after all.

The new porch addition was stunning, and now, finally, the pond and some new plants could be added. Ginny came by one afternoon and helped decorate while I set up the water feature and plants inside it. We laughed and talked about going on vacation together and leaving Tony at home so we would have a peaceful trip. And then we laughed hysterically at that, knowing quite well that Tony would go with us.

At the end of the day, my life felt in control again. My old rocking chair and a glass of wine, sitting on my porch, and one happy tear came down, but not mixed with my drink now. And I could, in time, take a friend up on his offer to go out dancing without feeling ashamed or afraid.

Chapter 25

Summer arrived, and I started hosting friends, sharing moments that made everyone feel welcomed and happy. My friends loved the new renovation, especially the sectional sofa, which was a hit. Someone joked about adding a television, and I quipped that islands don't have them. The husband then said, "Well, they usually don't have electricity either." That fun evening led to an invitation to their Fourth of July cookout, and that did sound like a tremendous amount of fun.

Things were looking up, and I planned to work out of town by month's end. There is always excitement when given the chance to visit New Orleans for a week, one of my favorite spots for photography. The lively crowds, incredible music, and delicious food make it an ideal place for me anytime.

In the meantime, photo shoots of weddings or birthday parties took place, and more requests for Senior graduation photos for students. I call these fill-in spots because my real love is nature photography. My second choice is being a street photographer, and that can be entertaining at times as well. Once, I asked two ladies jogging if I could take photos of them as they raced down a path. The younger lady told me no because her behind was not big enough yet. I responded with a smile and a quick, "It's okay," which made her laugh. Another time, I asked a beautiful couple if I could take their photo while they sat on a park swing. The answer was a blunt "NO," and the lady explained how this was not her husband. It was hard not to laugh as I walked to my car, because her words were amusing.

Animals fascinate me as well, and usually they stay still. A lady once asked me to photograph her prize poodle in her garden. As we set up, a large cat leapt over the fence, and the chase began. Over an hour later, the two of us captured the dog, who was now covered in mud from the chase with the cat. No photos that day, but all the laughing and running made me sore from being out of shape.

The Fourth of July came, and I was excited to go to my new friend's home to celebrate. There were people everywhere you could see when I got close to their house. In fact, there were so many that you had to park on the main road and walk down their driveway to the celebration. These kinds of gatherings are fun to me, and I'm always more comfortable in a crowd than with a few people.

Pigs had been roasting on cookers for days, one of the partygoers said, and the smell was divine. Any food required for a good barbecue was there, all under giant tents. A band was setting up, and children were running everywhere, while being scolded about staying away from the food.

I recognized a few couples there, and so it was nice to see so many happy faces. Bringing my camera was a good idea to capture this day of celebration. And a dog who stood incessantly barking near the foot of a tree at a cat won the most shots of the afternoon. The giant feline happily sat on a branch, licking himself as if he had proudly won that game.

Most of the guests seemed to have a significant other and children with them. Unless it's a crowd, I'm uncomfortable attending a private party by myself. Single men usually can spot a female by herself and move in for the "kill." And if said female is new to the area, she is spotted quickly. It's almost like a game of hide and seek, with, of course, me hiding.

Two young ladies were sitting at a picnic table, and at least four men were around them. Poor girls, thinking to myself, I don't miss those days. Watching each of the guys strike out and then move on to find another victim at the party, I noticed a man who kept teasing these boys. This was his entertainment tonight, and the man didn't seem to be with his own companion.

We older people tend to do what he did, so we don't feel out of place being single ourselves. As I sat and watched the show they were putting on, it made me think about how short life is. Are we single because of a breakup or because we can't get along with a person long enough to be in a relationship? Or it's more peaceful being alone.

Summer went by fast, and life was getting back to normal. Friends continued to come by for a meal or to sit on Annie's Island and enjoy my new pond. Goldfish had been added, and their bright orange color was beautiful with the green plants inside the water. More than once, a squirrel came in through an open window to drink, and birds were occasional visitors.

Tony had brought a new speaker that could be wired into my sound system so that music could be heard on the porch. Playing Zen music and listening to the bubbling water in the pond was so peaceful. Ginny teased me often about not being able to dance to anything but country music, which I didn't like at all.

The quiet sounds of nothing at night were the worst, and so I had adapted to leaving the television on most of the night. Changes had come into my life in the last year, and it was a must for survival.

I had only been on one date since Evan's arrest, and it was pleasant enough. The same guy had texted me again and asked me out, but I wasn't ready for that, or anything in particular. Mostly, being left alone could be handled better than a man in my life.

Work carried me out of town for a few weekends, and I had not been to a bonfire at Ginny and Tony's in a while. But the weekend came, and finally I joined them and some neighbors for food and singing around the campfire.

At the end of the night, Ginny asked if there was any word from Evan. This was something we hadn't talked about in months, and I didn't want to now. Finally, there was a need to tell her about the second cell phone found after his arrest, the texts and photos of the women, and a few from Jessica.

Ginny and I went inside and sat down. Tony and the few people left were still outside, so we could talk in private. And then the words

I had never heard from Ginny until now: "Evan and Jessica were engaged, and he broke up with her to use you so he would have a way to go to work."

Holding Ginny's hand as it trembled, as she continued, I felt numb inside. Earline had talked to Ginny and Tony shortly after Evan's arrest, but they couldn't bring themselves to tell me. I would have to understand their reasoning on this, because Ginny was asking me for forgiveness now.

Jessica told Ginny that she knew about the second phone and that the women were all used for Evan's benefit. Ones that he knew before, during, and after his prison sentence for rape. Jessica also said that he was seeing other women while living with me. These women would meet him on his dinner break at work. And... the worst fact of all, Jessica and Evan had sex whenever I dropped him off at his mother's house. Ginny said some girl had dropped Evan's clothes off at Earline's house, so that's why Jessica left those two boxes on my porch. She knew where I lived because she had followed us.

When I got home, it was later than usual, and I felt relieved to know so much after it all. There was still a deep sickness inside me from everything Ginny had told me tonight.

Noticing the basket of leaves on a table beside my front door, I picked a few up when walking inside. And there, among the red ones from the cabin we had stayed in, was the skeleton leaf. Placing it on top of the others, I opened the main bedroom door, which had not been opened in months, and lay down on the mattress. I closed my eyes, took the pillow that had been Evan's, held it close, and thought about our first night at the cabin.

During the night, I woke up, having dreamed of him and our closeness. Not opening my eyes, but saying the exact words I had so many times before, "make love to me, Evan." And when the daylight came, I was wet with sweat, and my body ached for more.

How do you cry away the tears? You don't...

Chapter 26

There is nothing worse than admitting to myself that I had spent most of the night with a ghost. "That takes the cake, Annie." I didn't want to be human with feelings, wants, and needs. But my emotions were rampant when I lay on the bed, and not one thought of why my world had fallen apart.

Female: the better species in a relationship. "I like that," thinking out loud. Many years had gone by, and I had lived without a "male," but my oh my, how those desires would kick in from time to time, and weakness from sheer stupidity.

Before Evan, I rarely accepted dinner invitations. And no one spent the night at my home or stayed for a period of time. It was just not my lifestyle, since work took me out of town a lot. So how in the world had I ever survived the chaos that went on for months after the world of Evan Lang?

Perhaps I should become a Catholic Nun, or move to a monastery in another country! Yes, I could do that, and insanity would definitely set in because of the admission of being female.

"You can do this, Annie," I would repeat several times a day until no more feelings of any kind could be felt. Strong woman, good woman, unkept woman, better than this woman made sense to me. My new mantra!

So, every morning for months, when I sat up in bed, those words were repeated at least ten times. Living in peace was the only goal, and trying to achieve it was tough at first. Hate, fear, and the thought of what I had allowed to happen, right under my nose, made me sick.

The one thing that had been taken from me was self-worth. Counseling was not my idea of help, and not many friends want to hear your problems, especially concerning relationships. I was so thankful again to Ginny, who had stood beside me for several years.

I loved my work, and with a laptop, camera, and a suitcase in tow, many days were spent out of town. New people, places, and situations beckoned my soul to come and see what I could create.

The opportunity to visit my favorite island off the coast came again. The same house was offered due to a cancellation. A two-week stay, starting the week of Thanksgiving. Ginny was disappointed that I wasn't spending it with them this year, but she and Tony understood.

While reading the local newspaper a few days before I left for vacation, an obituary caught my eye. It was Earline's, and told of her having battled cancer and would be buried next to her husband in a Northern state on the Canadian border. And then the family that was left behind was in the obit. I read it twice before realizing that it said Evan Lang and his wife, Jessica. And it told their residence was in another state, far from mine.

All I could think of was that part of my life was over, and the scums from the earth had moved. But the biggest witch of all had succumbed to her due justice.

No longer would I ask for answers, nor care about the evil others had placed upon me. The whole situation had been a nightmare indeed, and only a strong woman could endure such a tragedy. Making peace with myself and keeping a promise to do so would be my forever life, from this day forward.

The ocean was blue while driving across the bridge to the island, and I sat with a glass of wine on the beach once more that day. Sunsets are magical and ask nothing of me except to enjoy their spectacular sight.

A new gift shop had opened close to the restaurant here on the island. Baskets were still a must-buy for me, and a few were purchased to fill with more seashells. Walking down the path to the beach house with baskets in each hand, a cat started to follow me. It was young, maybe six months old, and begged for my attention.

Expecting the kitten to be gone by bedtime, he was still sitting on my porch. Searching the kitchen and refrigerator, there was enough lunch meat along with milk to make this sweet baby happy. After going to bed, his sweet meows could still be heard at the door. He may be lost, and I would look for his owners in the morning. And so, the kitten decided that my bed was his for the night, and we slept well.

Morning came with the sun shining through the window. The kitten was still asleep on my pillow and happily purred when I touched him. By the time breakfast was ready to eat, the silly kitten had jumped on the table. He loved the oatmeal with milk and sugar, and ate as if he were starving again.

After breakfast, with the kitten on my heels, we set out for the store on the island. When I opened the door, the owner laughed and said, "That cat needs a home." And then told me how a cat and two kittens were dumped on the island. The other two had found homes with vacationers and had left with them. And this baby needed a home and undoubtedly had chosen me. The store owner's wife spoke up, saying she had never seen anyone pet this kitten, and that it must love me, given that.

As I collected shells, the cat chased tiny crabs on the beach and tried its best to avoid the waves coming in. Every step I made, so did he, and happily enjoyed his newfound mother, if only temporarily. With a sleeping kitten on my lap while writing, the realization came that he had gained weight. He was always ready to eat and didn't mind leftovers or anything from a can. We had become a team, and even when I showered, he happily waited on the bath rug.

He was my companion, so I bounced ideas off him while writing. I knew it had his approval from the louder purrs. Late afternoons, we would walk together and watch the sun fade into the water. I'm sitting on the sand, and he's in my lap, trying to sneak a sip of the wine in my glass. Everything about this kitten made me smile, especially how he has warmed my heart and listens to my words so intently.

A few times, we walked to the restaurant, and the kitten would sit on a bench outside until I came back. The leftovers from there were his favorite, and he ate with vigor when presented with seafood. I had begun to sing to this little creature at night while sitting in the chair on the porch. And knowing this calico kitten loved me, only because he had chosen my heart to love him, was totally acceptable.

Soon after sunrise, I loaded all the new baskets of seashells, along with my luggage. Checking one last time to make sure nothing was left behind that was mine, and the kitten was outside. I would miss my new companion and, at last, had made a friend who never disagreed with me.

Looking around, the kitten was nowhere to be seen, so I assumed he had moved on after he ate his last meal this morning. Opening the car door to leave, the calico kitten jumped from the backseat and startled me. "Hey, little beauty, I was looking for you!" Instead of getting out, he sat in the passenger's seat, as if to say, "Let's go."

What do you do when something so precious decides you are its new mama? You stop at the store on your way off the island and, since it's not open yet, leave a note: "The calico kitten has decided to move to the city with me." He has happily seated himself inside my car, and we are on our way home. See you next time, Annie. P.S. I decided to name him George, after the island.

Going across the bridge, George leaped upon the dashboard, as if he needed to see where we were going. He didn't act scared or concerned. At the end of the bridge, he jumped back into the seat. "You ready to go home, George?"

The trip back was never one I looked forward to. This new baby may help ease the loneliness and give me something to take care of. He was the cutest after all, and we had formed a bond that made "George" my family.

I would need a few things like food, cat litter, toys, and an appointment at a veterinary clinic. And I would take Ginny up on her offer of feeding this kitten when work would take me out of town.

Making it back home, the kitten ran in the door as if he knew where he was. And then, checking things out, he found my biggest potted plant near the French doors and used it as his bathroom. "George!" I yelled with shock. It had been a long time since a pet of any kind had shared my space. But how could I resist this calico kitten that had me talking to him as if he were human?

Chapter 27

A quick trip to the grocery store gave me everything George would need, and on the way back, I called a veterinarian. Having a cancellation two days later was perfect for his appointment, and the costs of vaccinations plus neutering were not nearly as expensive as imagined.

That night, I called Ginny to tell her about adopting a kitten. "Sounds like he adopted you!" and she laughed loudly. She reassured me that George would be taken care of while working out of town. No doubt Ginny and George would get along fine. Tony was not fond of felines, but knowing him, this one would be eating out of his hand soon.

The day came for George to take his trip to the veterinary office, and as always, he loved the ride. A neighbor let me borrow her pet carrier until I could buy one myself. That was a great idea, because when we arrived, there were two small dogs in the waiting room, and one did not care for cats, to my dismay.

The wait wasn't long, and after talking to the receptionist about the arrangements, I was told to pick him up in the morning. Poor George, he had no food or water after 11 pm the night before; he had to be starving by now. Whispering to George about not being afraid and "Mama loves you," a tear was quickly wiped away.

Almost an hour after getting back home, my phone rang. The receptionist told me that the doctor needed to speak with me and put me on hold. A few minutes later, the veterinarian told me my pet was a healthy, approximately 8-month-old female cat. And the shocker... she is pregnant. I was surprised and a little confused because how could my sweet little kitten be a mama?

Admittedly, Annie is a little slow at times. Okay, a lot of times.

I hurriedly put my shoes back on and raced out the door to retrieve my "male" kitten. When I arrived, the receptionist showed me to an examining room. The veterinarian came in with George in the carrier and asked me if he had the right cat. Agreeing that it was indeed my calico kitten, he was taken out of the pet carrier for me to hold.

I felt like a complete idiot, answering his questions. No, I had not examined the cat myself. Yes, I assumed it was male because I was told it was. Pregnant??? How did that happen? "No, Sir, I've only known this kitten around 3 weeks," but felt embarrassed.

I took George and sat down in a chair in the exam room. Asking as many questions as my mind would allow, with me being in shock, we proceeded. Telling me that George was going to have two, maybe three kittens in a few weeks, and it would be best to let "her" give birth to them. And then, when the new kittens are 6 to 8 weeks old, George could be spayed.

My sweet little kitten was going to be a mama, and I cried, overwhelmed by the unexpected turn of events. "Oh, George, what have you done?"

It was late in the year for kittens, which made me realize how unexpected this was. Cats usually have them in the Spring, so this puzzled me. Will there be signs when George goes into labor? GEORGE...that's a boy's name! I had not even thought of that. The veterinarian's words confirmed that the calico 'kitten' was pregnant, which made the situation even more surprising.

"Ginny, George is pregnant," I anxiously said on the phone. "A man can't get pregnant, Annie," and then came that loud laugh of hers. So, we talked about all the cats she and Tony had owned over the years, but none of them had a boy's name like mine.

George and I lie in bed at night, and she is visibly becoming bigger, and the fact that it was not just the food she ate on the island. Reaching over once in a while to rub her belly gently, she would roll over on her back. How sweet she was, and I wondered if George realized soon, we would have a larger family in our house, filled with love.

George acted as if visitors made her nervous, and she would pace in front of the bedroom door. Not knowing exactly when her new babies would arrive, I made her a beautiful bed with blankets in a large basket. Being beside my bed would make her feel comfortable, I thought. Several times during the night, sounds of her crawling into the basket and rearranging the blankets were heard. Something my neighbor told me that expectant cats do to prepare for labor.

During the day, George liked to lie in the sun on Annie's Island. Maybe she missed her old island home, and this was as close as she could get to the real thing. Her belly grew quickly, and it was fun to catch a glimpse of the tiny babies moving in her stomach.

By my supposed calculation, the birth time was getting close, so I tried only to be gone for an hour if errands had to be done. The babies inside her seem huge, and there were at least three now. Poor George, I don't know how she sleeps with so much activity going on inside her. Once, she bathed her stomach as if to calm the little ones, and she purred so loudly—a great mother she will make, and soon now.

On a stormy night at 11 pm, George began to make grunting sounds. About 20 minutes later, the same sounds came again, and the first baby came out slowly. Then I realized she was on my blanket, and not in the basket with her own bedding. Too late now, the babies were making their appearance.

A calico, a solid black one, and the third was a yellow, and George was a mama after almost two hours of labor. She cleaned them, and I did my best to welcome each one, with a bit of help from a warm, wet bath cloth. When she settled down, I took George and the babies and placed them in the basket beside my bed.

The storm raged on, but I finally dozed off to sleep with a hand on the basket lying beside the bed. The next morning, George woke me up as she bathed my arm. "You must be hungry, Mama," softly speaking to her. Looking over into the basket, I counted...one, two, three, four, five.... FIVE??

It had been at least four hours since the first baby had been born. And when that one was cleaned up, I moved them to their own bed, and George proudly nursed them all. We were both tired; it had been an exciting night, despite the storm. After taking the soiled blanket from my bed to the laundry room, sleep came easily with the sound of the rain outside.

I don't know what time, but by 9 am, when George woke me up, two more babies had been born. The three calicos looked just like her, and George was visibly proud of her newborns. Five tiny babies after all, and they were precious.

The days went by, and Ginny came to visit my new "grandchildren." George loved Ginny and Tony because they usually brought her cooked chicken. We would all sit on the floor next to the basket and pick up each baby so they could get additional love, too. Mama cat was always proud to show them off and would happily nurse the other babies while we held one or two.

Two weeks went by quickly, and a few kittens had opened their eyes. The basket was becoming too small for the litter, but to the best of her ability, George kept them placed back in there.

The kittens were fast becoming too heavy for George to tote, and it made me laugh to watch her gathering the rambunctious family. She was such an amazingly attentive mother and bathed them constantly. To watch them find things to play with was so much fun. Anything small enough for them to roll across the floor or pick up in their mouths, like a puppy, gave me fantastic photo opportunities. They certainly were a lively bunch, and along with eating soft kitten food, they had discovered the gold fish in the pond on Annie's Island.

After one of the kittens fell into the water while trying to catch a live meal, I placed a screen from an old window on top of the pond. One afternoon, looking out the French doors, George was nursing all five kittens on top of the screen—adaptation, I thought, with a smile on my face.

Chapter 28

With the word of 6-week-old kittens getting out, they all found homes quickly. Very satisfied with their new families, George and I were ready for them to move on, laughing about them. They had all become a handful, and my new drapes were in tatters.

It was time for George to have surgery, ending the kitten chapter and making it just the two of us again, living peacefully.

The day after George's surgery, I received a phone call from the owner of the tiny home on the island, with a surprising proposal.

Several times in past conversations, I had asked if he wanted to sell the little house on the island. He would always say his wife enjoyed the money, so the answer was no. Never thought he would be calling about selling two homes they owned, but here we were, and the price for both was perfect.

I told the homeowner to send me photos of both homes, and especially the one on the mainland. The images were stunning, and both remodels were amazing. He also said that he was not going to rent either home for the next month, so please come and look at both.

I was not ready for retirement, so the two homes would be an ideal source of investment income until that time. My workload was busy during the holidays, so I didn't have enough time to go to the island.

By the month's end, offers were made on both homes, and the owner gladly accepted. It was a dream come true for me; the tiny house I loved so much was mine.

Almost 8 weeks later, I finally had the time off to go down and look at my new investments. And of course, George was ready for another trip since she had not been on one since moving in with me. Once again, taking her front seat view, and away we went, to watch our daily sunrise and sunsets on the island.

George knew exactly where she was the minute the car door opened, and she took her rightful place on the chair by the door. After settling in, we took our walk to the store. As soon as the store owner saw us, he yelled out, "Hey George!" I told him the story about the kittens and how this male cat was, in fact, a "she." And then he told me there had been a stray male cat on the island, but he assumed it had left with one of the visitors.

A customer needed attention, so we didn't talk about me purchasing the little house that day. George and I walked quickly to the beach to watch the sun go down, and she chased tiny crabs once more.

Several couples on the beach watched the sunset and made comments about my cat. One young lady said she had never seen a cat on a beach before, and I told her this one felt at home here.

George and I trekked back to our tiny abode and called it a night earlier than usual. It had been a long day, and tomorrow was my trip to look at the house on the mainland. The air was cooler tonight, and the open window brought a welcoming breeze. It's always comforting to fall asleep to the sound of the waves coming in, and I dreamed about being on a boat out in the ocean.

The next morning came, and I had missed the sunrise. George insisted that it was mealtime, so we had our usual oatmeal with milk and sugar on top. George would have to stay here and not go with me this morning, but she would be fine without me. She would sleep on my bathrobe when work trips took me out of town, so bringing it with me was a good idea.

When I arrived at the larger home, a woman was standing in the yard. No one else was with her, and a car was parked on the street. She introduced herself as an investment buyer for a real estate company from a town on the East Coast. She was very knowledgeable about houses in this area and said she wanted to make an offer on my home and another down the street. Then she gave me her business card and told me to think about it and let her know the following week.

The renovation of the larger home was more extensive than the beach house. I loved the newer design, and from the photos the owner had sent me, it looked like a total remodel. Too bad this one wasn't on the island; the extra room would be nice there.

When arriving back on the island, I stopped at the store. The owner's wife was behind the counter, and she asked if George was with me. We laughed as I told the story of how he turned into a female. Both she and her husband were thrilled that I had bought the tiny house on the island and the home on the mainland as well.

Sweet George was waiting in the window at the tiny house. It's wonderful to be welcomed at the door with loud meows and her insistence on being held.

This year was the perfect time to write articles about beach life. I usually don't get to know anyone on the island, and that's a plus for me. The place of peace and work, in one, for me to feel rested upon leaving was perfect. That had always been my goal here, and thankfully, it's always been accomplished with ease.

When I left the store earlier, a dog was barking in the distance. People were courteous while vacationing here and kept their dogs on leashes. I don't know how George would react to a dog. There were none in my neighborhood now, since the older man had passed away.

Our usual walk to watch the sun go down is one of my favorite things to do with this crazy, but fun, feline of mine. Her antics are hilarious and amuse anyone else sitting on the beach. George loves the daily adventure and gets plenty of exercise running after crabs across the sand.

And then, out of the top of a dune, bolted a dog. Not a small dog but a large shepherd of some kind, with a man running behind him, leash in hand. The dog didn't bark but headed straight toward

George! I was in a panic far greater than my legs could carry me in the sand, and falling in the midst of it all, landing on top of my poor cat. The large dog ran past us and into the ocean wave, it went, with its screaming owner chasing after it.

Hurriedly, trying to recover my dignity as well as George's, I headed for my house. After tending to my scraped knee and feeding the now purring cat, I drifted off to sleep on the bed and across my bathrobe.

Morning came, and it was early enough to watch the sun rise. The man from last night was surely a visitor to the island, because I had not seen him before yesterday.

There is a feeling of invigoration that comes with the morning light, and the sun ensures that we are here, once more. It has always been my time to meditate and thank the Earth for letting me live another day. The beach on the island is perfect for that because locals don't wake up that early, and neither do most vacationers.

The tide had been high the night before, so the choice of a small, but dry, dune was a good place to sit. My knee was a little sore from last night's disaster, so I stood slowly.

In the distance was someone running down the beach, at the water's edge. The light shone on the figure, and then I knew who it was. Thankful that my sweet George was left on the bed this morning, I did a quick search of the beach, but he was by himself.

His hair was long with a golden glow from the sun, and his skin was darker than most of the usual vacationers on the island. "Where is your dog?" I asked as he approached me. "It was my sister's dog, and they left to go back home this morning," he replied. The man profusely apologized for what had happened and said with a smile that the dog was young and totally out of control around water.

"Do you live on the island?" he asked, looking out at the ocean. "No, but I just bought a home here," I answered, while staring at this gorgeous creature.

Chapter 29

We sat on the dune and talked about the island and its charm, which draws people here. And then the man told me that his parents were retiring and he had bought their business from them. A store, in fact, that was on this island, and he had moved here a few months ago. Having visited that store many times, I never knew the owners had children.

Saying our goodbyes, I began to walk back up the trail toward the little house. A place that readily felt comfortable enough to pour my heart into during every visit, whether lying in bed, sitting on the porch, or watching the sun on the beach.

"Hey, what's your name?" he yelled. Stopping in my tracks, I turned around. He was handsome, and the light wind blew his hair against his shoulder. "Annie," I yelled back down the trail. "Do you have a name as well, Sir?" And by that time, he had joined me on the trail. "My name is Scotty," the man said with a glint in his eyes.

We walked together up and over the sandy trail, and when we reached my tiny house, he waved and turned to leave. I opened the door, and George ran out to greet him, as if she knew this man. "Maybe I should too," thinking to myself, as Scotty walked away.

Oh, the visions in my head, while lying on my bed after watching him walk away. Being lonely has its drawbacks. And a long nap with dreams must have helped because the smile on my face later made even me blush.

"George, we need to go find your friend Scotty." But she didn't seem interested in anything other than the new cat food I had brought on this trip. Grabbing a shower and trying to look my best, with a new summer dress, out the door I went.

Walking to the store in the warm summer breeze made me feel young. Something about that dream had made me want the real thing again, but did I dare? At the last minute, the beach drew me in, and a dune beckoned to come and sit a while.

"It's always better not to repeat mistakes, Annie." And those thoughts kept going through my head repeatedly while sitting on the dune. What if he were an ex-convict, too? There would be no way my heart or soul could ever go through that again. My world had shattered into a million pieces, and how would I ever be in one piece again? It is truly something no one should go through. Knowing that humans are supposed to be good, regardless of what life throws at you, has been a challenge at times.

You know, this island has been good to me, and the second I cross that bridge, my very being changes. The weight of the world is gone from my shoulders, and even the things written here have a different tone. My world used to consist of TV news casts and daily publications, and this was before social media of any kind. But coming to see this beautiful blue water, watching the seagulls fly over, and seeing the scattering of tiny crabs is all so much more serene. The world has become a hate-filled place, and mostly because everyone is trying to rule over the other.

My morning meditation is full of love when I sit on a dune and feel the warmth of the sun upon me. That is precisely why my world has to be at peace, and this amazing island does that for me.

Today, there are visitors on the beach with their children. One is a tall woman with two little boys, who are full of laughter and mischief. The lady must be their nanny, because she seems short-tempered, I say, laughing. Not many people bring their children here, I've noticed. This island is more for grownups who enjoy the solitude and peace, like me.

There are more boats than usual this year—younger people who look like models ready for a magazine photo shoot grace the waters these days. I remember hearing about a lady who lost her million-dollar shoes while disembarking a yacht during a visit. Now that must have been an interesting sight! She was probably a lot madder than the nanny who just got sand thrown all over her by the two rowdy little redheaded boys.

When arriving back at the little house, George was waiting impatiently in the window. The sweet kitten that had followed me here from the store on this island and had insisted that I adopt a "boy" cat, like him. And oh, how I had been fooled into thinking the most significant issue would be that he would spray my furniture and leave that horrible male cat scent. What a surprise it was to find out that George was a female and had babies on the way.

My life with a cat was better than ever expected, even with the rambunctious little demons, as Ginny had called them. More than once, a kitten was offered to her and Tony, but they would always come up with an excuse not to take one home.

The beach always feels more at home, especially in the summer months. And now, with a pet to share this house with, it feels more like a family here. It would be nice, though, to have more room inside and a bigger porch for us to sit on. The renovation included only new cabinets and appliance upgrades, but the structure itself remained relatively small.

Initially, the island house was chosen for its rental price and location, of course. Of all the places I have traveled, it is truly the most peaceful and quiet. New Orleans is by far my favorite place to be, despite the crowds and noise. One is excellent for writing, and the other for photography, but the sunrise and sunsets on a beach are that little slice of tranquility needed the most.

George is at home wherever I am, and being adaptable is a plus with me. Annie's Island is almost always where you can find her, except when she lets me know it's bedtime. The new pond has been a massive hit with this cat, and she sits on a chair beside it to watch the fish. Ginny often says this cat needs that kind of entertainment because she was adopted from an island out at sea.

There may be some decisions to make now that I own two more homes. And suddenly it all hit me!

Lots on either side of the tiny house were vacant, and though a second-story addition could not be built here, I could add on to the sides of this one. The realtor is very interested in purchasing the larger home, so I will see what her offer is for that one. That would certainly give me more than ample money for renovations. And then, there would be no reason for me to live in my present location. Oh, wouldn't George love that!

The store owners would know who to contact about these vacant lots. Expecting rain, I took my car to eat dinner and do a little shopping. There were quite a few people in the restaurant, many of them tourists. A vacant table in the back caught my eye. Most restaurants at home, my laptop goes with me, but that has never been the case here. When sitting here, the windows are enormous, and you can't help but look out at the ocean. By the time my food is served, it has begun to rain, so people-watching in the dining room, unnoticed, is fun.

An older couple near me was deep in conversation, and the woman seemed upset. I smiled once at her when she looked toward me, to say I'm here if need be. When the gentleman got up to pay for their meals, the lady sat there. Taking it upon myself to see if everything was ok, I walked over. They own a house on the island, and it is now for sale. Quickly, she told me of how they were moving to their daughter's town because her husband has cancer. The beach house would no longer be used, and they would need the money from its sale. Her emotions were sad, because they had raised their children to vacation here. After asking for my name and phone number, promising to call me tomorrow, the couple left.

I decided not to shop, since it was raining. Driving back to the little house, thoughts of that poor woman and what she was going through made me realize how short life is.

Chapter 30

The night was beautiful after the rain, and I wanted to take a walk on the beach. After being gone for a while, I'm sure that George would like to go with me to chase the crabs.

Sandy paths are wonderful on my feet, and I've noticed how much smoother my feet are after spending time here on the island. But tonight, the moonlight is not as bright, so I'll take along a pair of shoes.

When the beach is secluded, it gives you a sense of the magnificence it holds. The little bit of moonlight tonight glows on the water's edge, mixed with the ocean's foam. But it's enough illumination that no flashlight is needed.

This silly cat chases anything that moves, except the water. Once I tried bathing her, and she jumped from the sink, up a bookcase, and onto a beam in the ceiling. Not one drop of water got on this crazy cat, but I, in the process, looked like a drowned rat. When Ginny came by, a few minutes later, she accused me of swimming in the pond on Annie's Island. I'm not sure that Ginny was ever convinced of the truth in that scenario.

After walking some distance down the beach, a figure can be seen, and it's coming toward me. Quickly turning around, I step up my pace. If it had been daytime, my walk would have continued down the beach's edge. George came down a dune, and I picked him up while heading back to the path toward my house. At the top of the hill, a glance back toward the water let me know the person had gone further down now, and there was no longer a concern. There has never been a safety reason here, but I was by myself, after all.

Heading out to the store the next morning was a must. George even protested that there was no milk in his oatmeal this morning. With little cabinet space in this tiny house, food is bought only for a few days at a time. Poor baby, she's so spoiled!

The store on the island had everything needed for now, since I had brought extra supplies with me on this trip. George likes milk put on everything I feed her, so I'll have to take my car to the store today.

Poor George, she doesn't like it when I drive off without her. But believe me, this feline will protest in the morning since there is no milk in the refrigerator for breakfast tomorrow. Who would have thought that a cat could control my life like this one does, not me for sure.

The small store and restaurant seemed very busy when I pulled up. It's always good to see new faces here and occasionally get to know a few people.

The store owners were busy with customers, and, admittedly, I looked to see if their son, Scotty, was there as well. Not many men look like a god of sorts as he comes through the sunlight, but he certainly does. Maybe he would let me do a photo shoot with him if I could keep from blushing enough to work with him.

A photo studio might not be a bad idea on the island. It's not far from the mainland either, which would be a massive plus for running a business like that. Most of my work takes me away in the spring and fall, so that the island visitors might be a good idea for photos in the summer months.

Walking to the table with produce on it, a man's voice could be heard behind me. My face lit up brighter than a Christmas tree, or so I thought it did. "We have to stop meeting like this," Scotty said with that deep voice of his. And then he put his arm around my shoulder as if we had known each other for years. The warmth of his tanned skin felt nice on my arm, and it made me glow. "Are you always this cheerful, sir?" I said, not wanting to sound giddy.

Scotty followed me through the store as I did my grocery shopping. Occasionally, he would touch my arm, and a chill would consume me in a good way. We talked about him taking over the store from his parents, and he seemed thoroughly excited about the new venture. He was renting a house on the island, but would definitely be buying one soon, he said. We briefly discussed my plans to expand my home here and sell the mainland house. And, of course, he asked about George, who was undoubtedly heartbroken because I had left her to do my shopping.

With my shopping done, Scotty helped me load my groceries into the car. Laughing, he said there was a restaurant close by with excellent food. And then he told how eating alone is no fun, but would be much better if a beautiful lady joined him. I'm sure there was a massive smile on my face when the words 'of course I will' came out of my mouth.

We took the milk from my car and put it in a refrigerator inside the store's office. After all, George would be highly disappointed without his milk.

We both ordered a seafood dinner and a bottle of wine to go with it. Candles were on the tables, and it was such a romantic room, even though there were plenty of other customers there. The moon was full, and you could see the light on the water from the large windows. Scotty was mesmerizing for sure, and it was hard to pay attention to whatever he was talking about.

After a glass of wine, my confidence rose, and I touched his arm. It was the first time my face didn't blush, and his full attention was mine. For a few minutes, his eyes stared into mine. It was still hard to find words outside of a general conversation, but I tried.

Dinner with Scotty was exciting, despite several glasses of wine that tend to relax me. He was a great conversationalist and seemed to know what made the world go round. His travels working for a yacht brokerage company were extensive, and so he had never settled in one place until now.

We talked for a long time after our meal, and then the manager asked if we wanted dessert. Looking around the dining room, there were only the two of us left, and neither of us had realized it was closing time. I laughed and said that my groceries still needed to be taken home, and that my milk was still in the office refrigerator.

Scotty paid our bill, even though next week he would be the official owner of the building that held the store and restaurant.

"Would you like to take a walk with me?" he asked with that beautiful smile of his. There was no need to answer him, and Scotty knew it. My hand took his, and we strolled down the street covered by the blowing sand. His long hair caught the breeze when we stopped for a moment to look at the moon on the ocean's waves. I reached to touch the amber-colored strands bleached by the sun, and they hung far below his shoulders.

We walked the few streets here and then down toward the beach. The houses on this end of the island are the largest, and they are rented or owned by families. Scotty commented that it made the island look uneven, with only large homes on one end. "Maybe I should move my other two homes up against my tiny house to make it bigger since it's about halfway down the beach," I said, trying to sound funny.

And then Scotty talked about how a larger marina on the island would be great for yacht owners. "Oh my, maybe a rich lady could lose more shoes trying to disembark again," laughing my head off as I'm saying this. He had not heard the story of the wealthy yacht lady yet, but he was certainly intrigued by it. We sat on a dune and listened to each other's tales of life on the beach. And his eyes sparkled in the light, almost as bright as mine, while listening to Scotty talk.

There was a stronger chill in the air when we stood up from the dune. Scotty wrapped his arm around me, and I had not realized that we were actually sitting in front of the house he had rented. "Do you drink coffee?" He asked. "Doesn't everyone?" I answered him.

The house on the other side of the dune was quite large and modern. A light was on the second-story balcony, but it was dark at the ground-level entrance. "Let's go see if the coffee pot works, and I'll let you make it," and then there was that laugh of his that could make anyone smile.

Scotty told me how he never envisioned this new adventure as his life. A world filled with travel and work was all he had ever known. And then we discussed how that makes you not want a relationship, and certainly not marriage. "The only regret I have is not having children," Scotty said, looking away from me. His sister had children, and that crazy dog that liked water more than land.

We drank coffee and ate a piece of leftover cake he had brought home from the restaurant the day before. Scotty mentioned how nice the balcony was at night and how excellent the view was, too. "Let's go," I whispered, and set my coffee cup down on the table.

There was a blanket on a chair by the back door, and it reminded me of the one from my own home. He wrapped it around me, but stopped at the door and didn't open it.

Knowing what was going to happen if I didn't leave now, my heart fluttered, and the blush on my face was intense once more. His lips were warm and tender when they met mine. Scotty took my hand and led me down the hall to a bright-yellow bedroom. "Why does this room look familiar? Saying it to myself. "My bedroom is the same color," I finally said out loud to him.

One piece at a time, my clothes fell to the floor. Scotty never stopped kissing me, as his hands did all the work. How do you describe a person who consumes your body and wants your heart? Daylight came far sooner than I wanted.

Scotty walked me back to my little house later that morning. George was excited to see humans, even though we had left her milk in the store's refrigerator. "I have a lot of plans for us, Annie." And as he left the porch, my sweet little feline followed him. Scotty stopped, picked her up, and brought her back to me.

I watched as he walked down the street again before I went inside. A few minutes later, someone knocked at my door, and it was Scotty. "You know what?" He said with a sincere look on his face. "I need you, Annie."

Sometimes in life, things happen for a reason. My photography studio on the island has been an enormous success, thanks to Scotty and, of course, our George.

www.ingramcontent.com/pod-product-compliance
Lightning Source LLC
Chambersburg PA
CBHW050001040726
47599CB00014B/1169